Eight Days in May

The amazing life changing story about awakening to your best life.

BY: DR. JEFFREY A. NEEDHAM

PublishAmerica
Baltimore

ISBN: 1-4241-0191-3
PUBLISHED BY PUBLISHAMERICA, LLLP
www.publishamerica.com
Baltimore

Printed in the United States of America

Success

To Laugh often and much, to win the respect of intelligent people and the affection of children; to earn the appreciation of honest critics and endure the betrayal of false friends; to appreciate beauty, to find the best in others; to leave the world a bit better, whether by healthy child, a garden patch or a redeemed social condition; to know even one life has breathed easier because you have lived. This is to have succeeded.

-Ralph Waldo Emerson-

To Marni Middleton-Needham. I thank you for the truly amazing love you have shown me and for teaching me to give my heart to the world everyday. I am forever grateful for the inward journey you inspired me to take and for your incredible support of my dream of making this world a better place. You are without a doubt my soul mate.

Acknowledgements

I have been blessed to have met one of the most extraordinary individuals on the planet. Dr. Tom Preston. During my time with Tom he was able to open my eyes and my heart allowing me to create my very own steps in the pathway called life. I express my most sincere thanks and gratitude to Dr. Tom Preston for everything he has done for me, for chiropractic and for the world. You are an amazing being whose presence has definitely been felt in this life. I love and appreciate you. You inspired me to put my thoughts into print to inspire those the same as you have done for me. You have been a great teacher.

To my wife. Without your encouragement and support I may never have completed this book or pursued its publication. I can honestly say that we did it together. You are the major reason the story of "Eight Days In May" has been told. You are an incredible energy that I love so very much.

To Ms. Samantha Scragg for your continual patience and hard work in finding a place for this book to be brought to life. You are the computer genius and structural motivation that formatted this book so many times I dread the thought of counting. Thank you for your time, your patience, your energy and your ideas. Most of all thank you for all of your hard work and dedication.

I cannot forget Rolly Middleton. A man that taught me one very valuable lesson! In a world that appears mostly superficial on the outside give them everything you've got on the inside. To treat people the way you wish to be treated and let the rest take care of itself. Here's to being one of the kindest and most genuine people I have ever had the chance of knowing.

To the Chiropractic profession I will be forever grateful! I cannot deny the great power that exists in giving and serving the many people of my community in touching their souls. No other profession can offer what Chiropractic has given me. An opportunity to help people connect with their better health and their better selves through witnessing the miracle of the inner power we all share. I can only hope that one day I can return the favor.

Life is no brief candle for me. It is a sort of splendid torch which I have got hold of for the moment, and I want to make it burn as brightly as possible before handing it on to future generations.
-George Bernard Shaw-

Introduction

The map of our lives without question conceals the amazing potential for a never-ending journey that every single one of us is destined to travel the moment we are born into this physical world. For most that journey takes place on the outside the minute we become influenced about life from the various sources around us. Whether we learn from people like our parents, teachers, friends, family, religious figures, media outlets and society in general these resources lend a hand in shaping who we will be, what we will do and ultimately the things that we should expect to have in our lives.

With the relentless pursuit of perceived success our external experience becomes one with a foundation solidified in the attainment of things that are seen. As the visible measures become ingrained in our minds we continue unconsciously stumbling upon the many circumstances of life attempting to Be, Do and Have in the manner that the external world dictates. You see the illusion exists in chasing the ideals of measurable success that are primarily set forth by the influences of others. Due to the fact that we are constantly exposed to their perceived meaning in defining our lives we begin to initiate our very own race from the illusion that we fear the most. By living a life from the outside that greatest fear consists of never being "good enough" in the eyes of others. And this is why we have a world of people hoping, wishing and dreaming that someday, something will change. That the planets will align and the universe will at last provide them with a considerable "break" in life! What is bred from this is nothing more than the unconscious creations of humankind that we refer to as victims of circumstance, creatures of habit and those with bad luck or even no luck at all.

Is it any wonder why the planet appears to be lost, drowning in its own ideals? People blaming other people for their own misfortune! Nations engaged in war to preserve the teachings of the past. Individuals desperately seeking comfort in the unfulfilling emptiness of items that they believe have been eluding their success. Are you one of the many unhappy and unfulfilled people on this planet? A person whose focus is locked on a desperate search to fill the hollowness inside of you? Adamantly pursuing the elusive answers to change your life? If you are than I want you to understand that there is a better way to live.

You see the weight of your life isn't based on the job you have, how much money you make or the kind of car you drive. A true life cannot be measured by the accumulation of things. However, most people endlessly pursue things of so-called value only to be left wanting more in their attainment. The same also occurs in the failure to acquire such material items. No matter the outcome success or failure people are never satisfied. Coined a failure or a success you still perceive that there is more to have in the formula of your life. Ignored is the truth that it is the unseen facets of your composition, most notably your heart and soul that adds weight to your life while you physically live it. So I ask you how do you want your life to be interpreted?

An extremely thought provoking question I am sure for most. Indeed a question that many cannot answer. Also a hole that many attempt to fill by method of chasing the elusive answers! However, instead of searching on the outside you must come to know that everything you will ever need in your life is on the inside. What do I mean by the inside? Try looking deep inside the body you have been provided. To see your soul! The proverbial spirit that electrifies you into being the true person that you are! Essentially you need to connect with the real you and the power that comprises you to be able to rise above the circumstances that control your life. Then finally you will arrive at the consciousness that formulates you in recognizing that the weight of your life should be felt rather than be seen. It is an awakening from the inside that will open your heart to what truly matters.

My experience with the incredible consciousness that has ushered forth in my life cannot be described in words. However, I will be forever grateful for the light that has been cast on the former darkness that my life had embraced. All it took was the courage to put my fears of the unknown behind me while allowing my soul for the very first time to direct my life. I can only hope that the story of Michael Jamieson emulates the power of conscious awareness that we all possess inside of us. An amazing energy that we all have to offer to a world that so desperately needs to see more real people.

Personal transformation is entirely possible for anyone who desires to leave behind the unconsciousness of a seen world. Sometimes all you need is someone to open the window that is blocking your inner light from shining.

Then and only then will the world be able to see your inner secret for the first time ever.

Enjoy the read and let the words go beyond your minds comprehension. Let them touch your real self. Let them touch your soul. And never, ever be afraid to let the world see the real you! When you finally listen and speak from the heart you will know that your own inward journey has begun to take flight. Remember to be strong, bold and real in allowing the weight of your soul to be felt rather than seen.

The Road Not Taken

Two roads diverged in a yellow wood,
And Sorry I could not travel both
And be one traveler, long I stood
And looked down one as far as I could
To where it bent in the undergrowth;

Then took the other, as just as fair,
And having perhaps the better claim,
Because it was grassy and wanted wear;
Though as for that the passing there
Had worn them really about the same,

And both that morning equally lay
In leaves no step had trodden back,
Oh, I kept the first for another day!
Yet knowing how way leads on to way,
I doubted if I should ever come back.

I shall be telling this with a sigh
Somewhere ages and ages hence:
Two roads diverged in a wood, and I—
I took the one less traveled by,
And that has made all the difference.

-Robert Frost-

Table of Contents

Chapter One:
A Second Chance

"One can stand still in a flowing stream, but not in the world of men"
-Japanese Proverb-

As I lie flat on my back, unable to feel my fingers, my toes or anything for that matter all I could see was a cloudy, opaque light shining through the denseness of what I assumed were my closed eyelids. In the distance I could hear voices too numerous to identify yelling my name. "Mr. Jamieson can you hear me? Michael please wake-up! Michael can you hear me?" Where I was at that point seemed a little less obvious to me than the person I had become of most recent. Nonetheless, without the ability to see or respond my present state was somewhat a peaceful mystery. Knowing that I could still hear myself as well as those around me offered some kind of obscure security. The only priority I had at hand was to end the continuous question I kept asking myself regarding what had happened to me. The events leading me into the darkness that I occupied were completely wiped out. No recollection of any kind whatsoever. Just a blank space in time was all I was left to analyze.

However, the situation grew increasingly mysterious. Amidst the constant questioning of what had happened to me I sensed I was floating aimlessly toward the dim light that appeared to illuminate the end of a very small tunnel. My body was directed toward the dim light very slowly beginning to increase its speed of travel as images of my life began to flash before me. The image of my office appeared. The sign on my office door with my name in big, bold, black print reading Michael Jamieson I-Global Fund Manager entered the picture.

My career meant everything. I managed over $400 million dollars invested in a hedge fund consisting of a host of technology stocks that managed to survive the tech plummet of several years ago. Managing the fund was my identity. I was Michael Jamieson, a hotshot financial visionary who managed millions of dollars and growing at the tender age of 32. Almost unheard of in my line of business! For me, I was the talk of the town not only because of my youth but because I saw the future. After all, I made people instantly wealthy. With the idea of investing in technology stocks in a primarily stagnate market that was recouping from a nuclear holocaust that wiped out many companies at that time. A market where overnight billionaires became penniless.

I was a regular on countless financial television news shows. A veteran of every cover story for every financial newspaper and magazine. Who would have thought a 32-year old, father of one and husband to the most precious woman in the world. I had a great career managing one of the most prosperous hedge funds of our time for the most prestigious company on the planet. With Ivey League business degrees from Harvard and Stanford I made more money than I could ever spend. I had a giant mansion in the suburbs of San Francisco. An army of luxurious automobiles parked in my garage. I was on a first name basis with countless movie stars, financial gurus and industry powerhouses. My work was endless. My days began at 4 am, running seven days a week 365 days a year. I was lucky if I was spared a holiday at Christmas or Thanksgiving. The future of so many individuals depended on me. Not only the investors but also the people at I-Global. They took a huge risk to support my venture in its infancy. So logically there were expectations of me that had to be met.

I had access to corporate jets on the drop of a dime. The company helicopter was waiting if necessary to avoid looming traffic that could potentially impede an ever-important business transaction. A tailor would visit my office weekly to outfit me with the finest in Italian suits. An army of hair designers and stylists were accessible so I could maintain my hygiene without leaving the on goings at the office. I dined at the finest of restaurants and drank the best of whatever alcohol that could be bottled for any celebration. In fact, I was accustomed to the word "celebrate". And celebrate I did! Being on top of the world had provided me with fame, fortune and power. At 32 I had it all including the attitude to boot. I knew who I was. I let others know it too. I treated those below me like dirt thinking I was somebody special. It was a regular practice for me to conduct myself in this capacity every single day I crossed paths with my colleagues. What of that life now? I guess it didn't get me very far!

Suddenly, my floating frame came to a staggering halt. I was no closer to the narrow light then when I started in motion. The voices that were previously drowned out of my cognition soon regained their power. At that moment all I wanted to be able to do was respond to the echo of voices I could hear calling my name. It was like being trapped beneath the heavy burden of snow that conceals a human body after an avalanche. But I could not muster a response. Continually, I heard "Michael wake-up" or "Michael please wiggle your toes if you can hear me." I wasn't asleep! I was trapped in some unknown dimension where I lay paralyzed in peace while floating in space. In fact, I believe it was the longest period of time I actually spent with just myself alone in over 5 years.

The pressures of a demanding career consumed much of my time. However, I yearned for the notoriety it brought me. It was a rush for a kid like me to be a prodigal son amongst the elders of the financial industry. On any given day I had the power to turn thousands of dollars into millions with the click of a computer mouse. Nothing else could top that rush of excitement. I was addicted. An adrenaline junky of sorts! Living on the verge of life and death every day. The funny thing was I knew I would always land on my feet despite the ups and down of the stock market. So much in fact that my growing ego started to believe in my own immortality! This was my life. My story. The way it never should have been written. Michael Jamieson, superstar "money man". The "crust" of corporate America unable to move a muscle. Left completely alone with only himself to talk too. What the hell went wrong?

As time stood still I couldn't have told you if I was hot or cold as my tactile senses had abandoned me. I attempted to reach out, sit up but all movements were suspended. My body was motionless, heavy in time and space, unable to communicate with its parts. The only thing I did know at the time was that I was lonely. Also afraid! The world of unknowns is undoubtedly the greatest human fear…and mine also. I am not sure if it was the unknown, the intense quiet that all of a sudden ensued or the fact that I was completely lacking control of my situation for the first time ever. You see, I was always in control. And to be in control in my business you were alone at the top. There aren't many people you can trust in the corporate world other than yourself. It's every man for himself. The stakes are high. The gambles even higher. Resulting in a mind harboring insecurities of the future and the fear of destruction. Communicating ideas to others could destroy your stature. The vision could falter. I trusted absolutely no one. I had no close friends. No real confidants in my life. In fact, up to the point of being lost in mystery I would characterize myself as a friend that no one would like to have.

It was this moment of reflection that preempted me to despise the person I had become. However, these feelings quickly passed in my recall of accounts of near death experiences. I remembered near death being described as a sense of calm. A world of silence in the midst of stillness. These coercing thoughts broke my previous sense of peace because I couldn't help but wonder if I was actually dead or alive.

My anxiousness increased as the dim light reappeared in front of my face yet again. It grew larger, more apparent as it neared closer. At first it was dusky like the dullness of the moon on most nights. However, it characteristically appeared to be transforming into a bright yet radiant object. More so, like the sun. So was I actually dead? Is this death I repeated? Because if this was death I didn't like it! What could be worse than feeling like you are encased in a buried coffin with only yourself. I think I would rather be dead than with myself. However, if it were seriously death wouldn't I have been more attentive to thinking about my family, friends, loved ones instead of only me? I pondered this question and felt in some way I should sense a feeling of loss for the truly important people in my life that I left behind. But I didn't. Contrary to this theory all I could envision was myself, my future, my life. It was all "Me". The evolution of the narcissistic creature I had grown to become. Overwhelmed with selfishness.

As the pondering became old I reverted my attention back to the voices that once again seemed to be amplifying around me. They not only gained volume, but clarity. "Mr. Jaimeson, can you hear me? Please wake up! Move a finger if you can hear me! Wiggle your nose or blink. Please anything." The voices grew not only in sound but also in frequency. It was overwhelming as I heard one plea after the next attempting to make contact. The speed of the voices started to accelerate also. I remember them sounding like the usual group of financial reporters that bombarded me daily looking for answers to their questions regarding the day's economic outcomes. I hated those events then and most certainly was annoyed by them now.

The voices, the sounds, the frequency and the speed all seemed to escalate entirely out of control. Beyond my capacity to even comprehend. And as they did I felt a rush of tension throughout my entire statue of a body. I broke down bracing for what I believed was the end of my existence. I believed amongst the sensory attack I was sustaining that I began to shrink in the space I occupied. My body initiated a sense of spinning violently as if I was being sucked down some type of drain. It felt like it was almost goodbye. In conjunction with the physical plight my body was participating in the overwhelming auditory perception I had experienced became sonic in sound. The intense volume accompanied my spiraling frame on its journey into the unknown. In an instant a deep darkness eclipsed my vision for what seemed like an eternity. In the moments of darkness the tension of my body intensified as the air was siphoned from my lungs. I was gasping for breath as nothing but fear ran through my veins. I remember the onslaught of images of my life. Up to that point the pictures increasingly drowned me as the darkness completely dominated the previous sounds.

All dark, all quiet that's all I remembered! It seemed that everything had hit a plateau. As I was drowning in the images of myself I managed to commit to making one last effort to supply my lungs with air. I squeezed my chest as hard as I could and opened my mouth with great force to get a breath of air. It was then that I awoke gasping, engorged with the bright light of a hospital emergency room, accompanied by what seemed to be a herd of medical technicians surrounding me. I was alive! I was finally able to wiggle my toes, blink my eyes and make a noise. Everything that everyone on the outside world had asked me to do I could finally accomplish. So now one question was answered. That being whether I was dead or alive. But I still needed one more elusive answer. What happened to me? In that moment all I could remember was leaving the collapsing darkness that was absorbing me to enter into the explosively loud white light that seemingly flushed me back to reality, as I knew it. It was then that I heard the words "Thank god, your alive. Welcome back Mr. Jamieson. You gave us all quite a scare."

Reflection

"There is no object so foul that intense light will not make it beautiful."
-Ralph Waldo Emerson-

As I popped many a cork on the team of bottles of expensive champagne my staff of analysts, brokers, traders and marketing assistants all raised a glass to toast the day's triumphs. It wasn't an uncommon experience to celebrate small victories each step of the way. The majority of the festive occasions took place right on the I-Global battlefront. There was access to whatever was necessary to entertain a client or throw a party. And that is what I did to put a little fun in the lives of the many who sacrificed themselves for the funds success.

Every month orders were placed to maintain a full stock of items such as scotch, champagne, vodka and gin. You name it, we drank it! The cases of celebratory poison were stocked at the full serve bar in the executive lounge on the 21st floor. In fact, every executive had a healthy relationship with the finest distillers at the wet bars in their office suites.

On this day my staff and I met in the executive lounge at the close of the stock market to pay homage to the financial gods for the successes we had in making a substantial monetary gain on a high risk venture in China. Out of all the fund managers I used the suite the most and why not? Not only was it fully stocked with the best of booze, hor'derves could be ordered through the use of the corporate chef. There was a world-class selection of cigars in a humidor with a state of the art ventilation system. The sound system was out of this world. So this is where we partied hard at the end of a grand fiscal day.

The parties were a riot. Tons of booze, smoking and strategizing kept the troops loose yet motivated for the days to come. As the cocktails were flowing endlessly the inhibitions seemed to dwindle as the music climbed in volume. Suit jackets became friendly with the back supports of company chairs as ties were tossed in every direction. Shirt buttons were undone a couple of notches as I-Global transformed from prestigious financial institution by day into a yuppie watering hole by night.

It wasn't long until the real decadence of the night arrived. With the toasting of China, the pumping of the music, the stash of all stash had found its way to the party. It was pretty regular that some synthetic substances other than alcohol hit our cerebral senses and this night was no exception. As I gazed up from the confines of my drink to observe the events surrounding me I could see staff members dancing on tables, drinks spilling due to lost coordination, smoke rising to the ceiling and mass flirting taking place amongst co-workers both young and old. Now this was a party I thought. And several nights a week this is how I lived my life. One big party! If it wasn't at the office it was at some local establishment in the big city. Thank goodness the walls of the executive lounge were sound proof for my team parties because they were sure to be brought to a halt by the other executive fund managers still burning the midnight oil.

As I poured another scotch I looked down in front of my glass on the bar to see three distinct lines of beautiful powder. Ah yes! One of my fondest leisure time activities had begun. I always said, "Misery meets company". And the cocaine was stellar. In a matter of 30 seconds the lines of white bliss entered my nasal passages on the journey to numb my cognitive senses. My world was fast paced. So I had to keep up. Sure it was hard work getting power and prestige but it was even more difficult in keeping it. Make no mistake the company I worked for had goals and bottom lines. If these weren't accomplished it didn't matter how good you were today because you were expendable tomorrow.

The talent pool in the business world was deep with everyone gunning for your demise. There was no length that people wouldn't go to compromise their integrity, values and principles to succumb to the all mighty dollar and its advantages. Everyday my life was pressure packed. Not only managing money but also thinking one step ahead of the pack of wolves following in my footsteps. I did a lot of worrying coupled with thinking every second I could. My mind was a cosmic meteor shower of ideas shooting back and forth. This alone could have been considered my greatest weakness. It could wear even the toughest of souls down. And where me down it did. Everyday of my life I was a basket case on the inside. An utter accumulating emotional wreck!

No question I loved the rush attached to the potential risks involved with the volatility of money. Either making the coffers grow with outlandish trades or losing it with tainted advice from misleading insider scoops. Everyday was a high of sorts in the land of the unexpected. However, I spent most of my time looking ahead. Always a step ahead of the rest! With all the peaks and valleys of a regular business day coupled with the demands of my life I turned to what I believed to be performance-enhancing substances. No, not always alcohol! Liquor was primarily an after hours love affair. I meant cocaine, speed and painkillers. That's why it made perfect sense to me as to why I would spend countless hours on the 21st floor pounding back an endless supply of scotch, snorting cocaine and contemplating screwing one of my personal assistants.

The days and even the nights were a constant blend. A rush of one night overlapping the next. It became a lifestyle for me. One I grew to love. And one

I became dependent upon. I felt it was my escape yet also my advantage. As I polished off another drink the next full glass in line awaited my attention. Another three lines of bliss went up without resistance. It was a rush of a different kind. A whole other world than the one I was living in at that time in my life. An escape if you will. It was mine! Built by yours truly. One that I had full control over. No one in corporate America could sober me up or pump the chemicals from my body. It was this physiological alteration that enabled me to become something other than Michael Jaimeson. It was a shelter from the onslaught of pursuing predators that I felt every second of every day.

More booze, more blow. This is how I lived by night. At least I think I did. It kept me fresh and ready the very next day. It's almost as if I had visions for the future while I was in this altered state. A place of internal wisdom and safety! It must have been as I awoke the next day on the lambskin sofa in my office at I-Global wearing the exact same suit as the day before. Something that I rarely got excited about! That was the reason I kept a spare change in the executive restroom. In collecting myself from the previous nights events I remembered slowly maneuvering to find the phone. I called for a coffee and a copy of the morning paper. Time to start my day. Long before the prowling wolves, of course! It must have been one hell of a night? I use to think either the booze or the drugs would wind up killing me but the larger my ego grew so too did the feelings I had regarding my own immortality. I felt as though I was going to live forever. Not only was my body toxic but so too my mind.

Chapter Two:
Heaven or Hell?

"The mind is its own place and in itself can make
a heav'n of hell, a hell of heav'n"
-John Molton-

Over the course of what appeared to be a week or more in the hospital crisis unit, I spent the majority of my time sleeping. The remaining hours were delegated to internal torture by way of contemplating my past life hoping the future looked brighter. I still had no inkling of an idea as to the preceding events that led up to my admission to the hallowed halls of the sick care institute I inhabited. I was eager to find out the details of my sudden admission. Daily I attempted to recall my recent past but none of the answers were revealed. Part of me was dying to know but the other half mysteriously feared the answers. Not a day passed where an orderly, nurse or doctor briefly entered my room that I interrogated for answers regarding my arrival. However, the orderlies knew nothing, the nurses all changed the topic and the medical doctors were mainly interns lacking the social skills to answer such a personal inquiry.

So the question I longed to understand remained a definite unknown for the time being. Instead, I furthered my quest of self-analysis by reflecting back to my experience in what seemed like near-death. In reality, it was all I had to do. My body was exhausted. I had difficulty moving my limbs. Any movements I did have brought me to fatigue relatively quickly. I felt like vomiting at least twice an hour and all that appeared to be functioning properly was my head. I was never one to believe in heaven or hell but that view was beginning to change. All of my time spent alone in the mysterious darkness seemed more like heaven than waking up to a chaotic hospital environment, which didn't at all promote the angelic peace I thought it might.

Even in the land of the living I was totally alone. I had access to out-dated magazines but was too tired to flip the pages. There was no television, newspapers or radio present for my cognitive amusement. All I had were those pictures from the past that lie deep in the memory chip of my mind. The nurses constantly checked in on me. Unbeknownst to me there was also a security camera monitoring my every move above the doorway. On numerous occasions I wondered what it could possibly be used for. If people were interested in observing my exciting experience trapped in a hospital bed they must be bored. A big day for me usually encompassed making million dollar business deals all over the globe. Instead, I was downgraded to the painstaking task of attempting to walk ten feet to the restroom to relieve myself. That alone was a workout like no other. The funny thing was that going to the men's room was something I had very little time to do during my regular life. Yes, it became clearer! I was indeed in hell. Alone, feeling sorry for myself. Held hostage in a bed I could barely move from. Tampered by the vicious sponge baths provided by a full figured nurse named Ida. Please, somebody give me some answers!

"Hello Michael," a friendly voice spoke as I quickly opened my eyes.

"My name is Dr. Marshall and I am the Chief of Psychiatry here at County General. I have been observing your case since your arrival several days ago. Unfortunately, I have been backlogged with several emergencies, so I apologize for the delay in meeting with you."

Psychiatry! What on earth am I doing in a department like that? I asked Dr. Marshall.

"You mean to tell me you have no idea as to why you are here Mr. Jamieson," he replied.

No absolutely none at all. I mean I heard from afar that I nearly died, but the details are a little sketchy. Perhaps you can fill in some blanks Dr. Marshall, I said in a charming tone.

"Okay Michael. Here goes."

"Precisely three days ago you were found passed out, unresponsive, near death in your car while it was still running in the middle of traffic on Beaver Dam Road. Lucky for you an off-duty police officer took charge of the situation by administering CPR to you until the paramedics arrived. That is how you ended up at County General Michael," he said.

That's the story? I asked hoping to hear more.

"No, there's a little more to it. At County you crashed the moment you arrived at the ER."

Crashed! What do you mean by that? I said in fear of the answers.

"Your heart stopped beating Michael and the ER crew had to work to restore all of your heart and lung capacities."

So I almost died?

"At the time they also had to figure out what caused your near death events. So a series of tests ensued. The blood toxicity screen filled in the details for us. Michael your blood stream had enough cocaine and amphetamines in it to paralyze an elephant. You quite simply overdosed. Let me also mention that you are extremely lucky to be alive today because of that."

So how does that get me into the psychiatric ward? I muttered.

"I was hoping you could help me, Michael," Dr. Marshall replied.

Help you? I haven't got the foggiest idea about any of those events, I said.

"Well the police have been investigating your case. They are anxious to talk with you regarding a few details."

The police! What do they want with me?

"Consider the scenarios for a moment, Michael. Being found in your car like that could follow several plot lines. Foul play is still something that is very much a possibility."

You think someone tried to kill me? I asked in obvious disgust.

"It's either that or you've been inhaling illegal substances at your own free will," he replied.

I shook my head for a moment before saying, Try to kill myself?

"So help me out here, Mr. Jamieson," Dr. Marshall pleaded.

What do you think happened to me Dr. Marshall?

"My take is that you have a serious addiction to dangerous substances. However, until discussing this with you a couple of loose ends still need to be tied up. Someone could have tried to kill you with an overdose. You also could have tried to kill yourself. Or you simply had too much fun partying that night and your body shut down."

And these are psychiatric concerns? I questioned.

"These are both a personal and psychiatric issue," he replied.

So, why the ward?

"We needed to keep a close eye on you until we had some answers. This being said you could try to kill yourself again. You might be in personal danger. Maybe attempt to leave. These are all possibilities. Strictly for your own safety of course."

I pondered the scenarios mentioned by Dr. Marshall. Well, for starters I can tell you this. Nobody tried to kill me. Including myself!

"So you are obviously a drug user? Dr. Marshall said.

Don't you know who I am?

"Other than meeting you today I have no clue," he replied.

I am a big time financial guru with tons of enemies but not a single one would try to kill me with quality coke and speed like the stuff you found. They would have likely used rat poison or something cheap.

"So these are substances you use knowingly?" he asked.

Things I like to call performance-enhancers.

"Oh, I see it now. You are without a doubt addicted to this stuff."

My career demands much of my time beyond anything you could ever imagine so lets just leave it at that shall we.

"Mr. Jaimeson with all due respect you are lucky to be alive as we speak. Scientifically, you are an anomaly. Quite frankly you should be dead, but some higher power beyond medical intervention overturned the destructive forces of your chemical dependency for some reason."

I hesitated before shouting; I do not have a dependency problem! I resent your remarks Dr. Marshall!

"Look, Mr. Jamieson. Call it what you want but you have a serious issue that nearly cost you your life. Do you not see that? You may not have been deliberately trying to kill yourself but indirectly living this way you are either going to wind up dead or killing someone else I assure you.

Dr. Marshall's last statement echoed through my mind like the explosive nature of a rumbling volcano near the point of eruption. He was absolutely correct. Living the life I was happened to be all I knew. It was my identity. However, I also knew something else. If being at odds with myself was hell than I needed a method to escape that reality. In that moment clarity came upon me to some degree. The choices were obvious. I could take the easy way out through suicide or create a heaven of hell by physiologically changing the person I despised. So I chose the latter. Through regular use of mind-altering substances like cocaine I became a different soul living in a far brighter world than the one I was in at present.

Since I was too much of a coward to actually kill myself directly I figured the easiest way to disconnect from myself was to alter my state. To quite simply visit another world! At least in this capacity I would have no conscious observation of the who and what I had become in my life. To further that I would also have no real awareness that I was dying a slow, yet easy death! I felt strongly that this was my best option for continued success. Most people could take a vacation from their lives. A step back so to speak. Not me! So this was my opportunity to escape all that consumed my life. Including myself. However, there was no way in hell that I would admit that to anyone including the likes of Dr. Marshall.

Look Dr. Marshall your synopsis is genuinely appreciated but what I do with my body, with my life is ultimately my choice wouldn't you agree?

"Mr. Jaimeson I suppose to some extent your accurate. However, when your actions and loss of better judgment begin to endanger not only yourself but others then that's when it's necessary for people like myself to intervene."

"Look Michael, if you want to destroy yourself, go right on ahead. But there are a great number of things to live for in this world. If you could somehow only see past yourself."

Dr. Marshall please spare me the counseling session. I have done a magnificent job at captaining my own ship thus far. There aren't many promising young executives like me you know. I am successful, wealthy and educated to the hilt.

"And your suffering from an illness," Dr. Marshall replied.

So when can I get out of here. Back to my life? I asked. The kind of normalcy I am accustomed too. You know things like reading the newspaper. Watching television. A computer perhaps? I have to get back to my business, I said.

There are a lot of people who will be worried about me! Can I finally see my friends and family? I asked.

Dr. Marshall raised an eyebrow and slanted the corner of his mouth in contemplation of how to address my requests in as less damaging a response as possible.

"I am not sure how to break this to you, Michael," he responded. "There is no one waiting to see you."

What about my co-workers? Hey what about my family?

"To my knowledge not a soul knows you're here. We have had no inquiries in this department at all. Not one regarding your sudden absence."

You mean to tell me that they aren't waiting for me outside? I said in disbelief.

"The truth is," he said with a pause. " I am sorry to tell you that you arrived here all on your own and not a single person has called to find out about your disappearance."

No one at all knows I am in the hospital?

"Michael, we called your residence on numerous occasions leaving urgent messages in hope that someone would return them. However, to date not one of our calls has been returned. As far as your employer is concerned, we had no idea as to who that was so it is doubtful they've been alerted to these events."

The office doesn't even know where I am? I shouted out loud.

"I can certainly have them contacted on your behalf Michael. We'll get right on that!"

You're kidding me with all of this, right? I said. This is some kind of oversight!

Dr. Marshall visually bit his lower lip. "No I'm afraid not Michael!"

I guess in the reality of what nearly caused my death I was a little shocked that the people in my life hadn't rushed to my bedside. However, in the grand scheme of things I was just another number on this planet. One that was so wrapped up in his own sense of self that nothing and no one else mattered. It was true when they said, "what goes around comes around". Part of me hoped to see my wife during my recovery, but Lisa and I separated four months previous to the event. She and our daughter Eva retreated to our beach house in Monterey. A sanctuary distant from the hustle and bustle of San Francisco. In this time the only contact with my wife was by way of bank transactions. I continued paying the credit cards and Lisa still had access to the bank accounts. These were the only regular reports that I received to know that my family was all right. This was the only confirmation I had.

As for my daughter Eva I thought of her often but usually due to the guilt that my newfound lifestyle evoked upon me. The images of my daughter usually showered my mind as I stared at the bottom of my empty glass or gazed at the ceiling while passing out on my executive sofa. I was overridden with guilt because of what I had become. I missed the innocence in my daughter's eyes. The pure, unrefined and secure look that I saw when I stared into those little eyes! Everything her father wasn't. It gave me a sense of security to see these images. However, I was saddened when I considered my separation from the two most important human beings that loved me.

You see, I left them behind! Maybe I knew I was indirectly toxic to their wholeness. However, I did not want them around my volatile life. Was it guilt on my part? I don't know! I believe it was more in retrospect a precautionary move on my part so they wouldn't have to witness my evolution into the monster I had become. Whatever my motive my immense ego was shattered as I lie in a hospital bed after nearly dying unannounced to the world. Even worse would be Michael Jamieson passing on without the only two people he loved at his bedside. How's that for a reality shock? Not to mention that my career at I-Global was up in the air while I was missing. I could recognize that my personal life was on the rocks. Obviously my health was in question but my career? If I lost my job that meant the end of my career and that spelt disaster! In my eyes nothing else mattered but my work. Not my family. Not my health. Not even "me." The reality was Mr. Michael Jamieson, unknowingly the super wizard of finance for the moment, but certainly life shattered beyond self-recognition. I guess deep down I knew it. However, what my head was thinking and what my heart felt were two significantly different things.

Lisa and Eva who characterized a large part of my life were gone. In a series of events I culminated on my own that I came to accept over time. On the contrary, I-Global was all I had left. I literally sacrificed everything in my life for that company. It was my sense of identity. If this was removed I was ruined. In fact, I could honestly say that the people who revived me brought me back to the uncertainty that was my ongoing life. Leaving me to die would have been a far greater choice. Instead, the dark cloud of myself still loomed over this world. I truly believed this especially when I looked at the family pictures in my office. The world needed more people like my wife and daughter and far less of people like me. Why on earth was I spared I thought in contemplation of the last several days events? Returned to the destructive life I was leading?

"Michael, the administrative staff is in the process of contacting I-Global as we speak to fill them in on the details of your accident. I have also taken the liberty of briefing the police on the unknown details surrounding your admission. Everything is taken care of from that end. In the next hour or so you'll be transferred to a private suite with television access. As for your health situation, you still have to undergo some testing to determine the possibilities of organ damage from the incident the other night."

So what about getting out of here? I asked.

"That all depends, Michael! The testing will shed some light on the matter. Plus, your only recovering from the crisis brought on the other night. We haven't yet witnessed the withdrawal symptoms that are going to storm into your world".

Withdrawal symptoms?

Dr. Marshall looked me straight in the eyes. "Yes, Michael! You are an addict! You are recovering nicely from an event that should have killed you. You are in absolutely no shape to be doing anything other than resting. Not only that, the physical and mental withdrawal symptoms that are looming will be a sickness in there own right."

So when can I leave? I taunted further.

"We'll see how the tests go later today and into tomorrow," Dr. Marshall replied.

And then? I stated.

"And then we'll see what happens."

Thank you Dr. Marshall I appreciate your time in this matter.

"Look Michael, you may see this as hell but I assure you that it doesn't get any easier from here on out. It doesn't have to be like this because the distinction between heaven and hell is a creation of your mind."

Dr. Marshall, with all due respect please don't shrink my mind with all the psychobabble!

"Michael, you need to rediscover the heaven that exists in all of us," He replied.

Yes, sure whatever you say Dr. Marshall, I interrupted.

"There are a number of programs that can be successful in helping you accomplish this, so please give it some consideration. I can even set you up with some fabulous people in the field of rehabilitation."

With that as the conclusion of my unexpected meeting with Dr. Marshall I retreated to the hollowness that was my own inner self. In my time with Dr. Marshall I was growing increasingly agitated, frustrated and impatient. I was uneasy, shaky and trembling uncontrollably. Whether that was the recovery or the withdrawal I did not know. However, amidst the changes in my health I continued the sort of self-torture I was accustomed too. The idea of my life tossed in a dumpster was becoming all too real. First my wife and daughter! Now my career seemed questionable. All of a sudden my existence appeared unstable. How was it that I dodged such a colossal bullet in life yet again? Was I just lucky or was some higher power calling the shots? The more I thought about the issue I concluded some higher form was trying to entice me to see things differently. It was my view on immortality that all of a sudden began to change.

Reflection

"The hardest challenge is to be yourself in a world
where everyone is trying to make you be somebody else."
-E.E. Cummings-

I met Lisa the first year of my MBA degree while attending Stanford University. The day I will never forget was the day I first laid eyes upon her. I remember being at the athletic building on-campus checking in for a workout with a classmate of mine at the time. While standing at the front desk waiting for a towel I crossed eyes with a stunning, 5'10, dark haired, green eyed, olive skinned knock out that rubbed up against me. She interrupted the staff for the keys to the aerobics studio on the main level. When the keys were passed over to her she dropped them at my feet. So naturally I picked them up and knew at that very moment it was love at first sight.

Over the course of the next several months I began to incorporate aerobics into my workout regiment strictly because Lisa was the head instructor. At first I was stealth regarding my strategy to pursue her. Of course it would have been too easy to just ask her out on a date. So I began to take her classes minding to only myself. However, it began to look pretty obvious being the only male in a primarily all female environment. My extreme lack of coordination demanded extra attention from Lisa. Something that she appeared happy to oblige! In doing so it allowed us to develop a comfortable rapport with one another. From that time on we regularly exchanged smiles, intercepted glances, made flirty eye contact and shared nervous conversations both before and after class. Anything I could do to appear as though I was more interested in aerobics rather than Lisa I tried. I did not want to appear as though I was badgering the innocent woman. It just had to feel right for me to know whether to ask her out. Finally, the vibe seemed mutual. During a class I approached Lisa and as we chatted I mentioned the possibility of dinner together. She accepted my invitation and openly concluded after that point she knew the only reason I attended her classes was to ask her on a date. I was busted. Caught red handed! It was also the last aerobics class I would have to take. That is when our love affair began.

In 1998, I graduated from Stanford University with a very prestigious masters degree in business administration. With Harvard falling by the wayside and Stanford behind me it was time to put those expensive degrees to practice. I wanted greatness. Part of that greatness included Lisa. So on the eve of my graduation, two years after finally meeting the woman of my dreams I accomplished the unthinkable. Over dinner with her parents and mine we discussed our prospects of the future. Before the final course arrived I made certain that both sets of parents had loosened their collars with enough wine in preparation for dessert. As the dessert orders arrived I stood on my feet to make a very special announcement. That same intimate family gathering for my graduation also became my wedding proposal to Lisa. At that moment the covered dessert tray sitting in front of Lisa was uncovered for her to view a black ring box containing the flashiest ring money could buy. It was the ring that would ultimately represent our future together. I proposed in an elegant fashion by dropping to one knee and she happily accepted. We were literally on cloud nine together.

Following my graduation I was heavily recruited to work at numerous financial houses in the San Francisco area. Considering the details of these offers I had much more in store for my future. So I took the first of many risks in my career. Instead, I chose anything but the prestigious firms that touted me. I decided to opt for a small Silicon Valley start-up company that was on the verge of explosive technology. And explode it did. In the height of the technology boom the company took off with a frenzy of interest. I was a big player in all of this. Quickly becoming the chief financial officer within the first several months.

As the year passed Lisa too had completed her studies at Stanford by achieving her PhD. In doing so Lisa accepted a teaching position at the University while I continued to move up the ranks at the now publicly traded Wall Street Company. As the year went on numerous analysts pegged the company as one of the hot stocks to buy. It became one of the fastest growing fiber optic companies in the world with new technology to change the face of world communications. The pace was fast and I loved every second of being in the middle of it. The companies growth exploded. We were doing deals around the globe generating millions of dollars for investors. I was ecstatic, passionate and purposeful during this phase of my life. Most of all I was alive in every sense of the word. However, little did I know my luck was about to change!

Later that summer Lisa and I were married in a fairy tale setting that took place overlooking the shores of the Pacific Ocean. We loved the Monterey Peninsula ever since we discovered it while attending school in California. So that is where we ended up saying those sacred vows together. It was Northern California that attracted us to spend many romantic moments. So it was a logical setting for Lisa and I to start our future there. It was the perfect place to celebrate our union as husband and wife.

Two months following our wedding the firm I was so involved in was in hot pursuit by a major telecommunications company. That meant a possible takeover bid was taking place. In the end it was through a hostile turn of events that my firm became absorbed by the larger predatory company. The result was the takeover was complete and we lost principle control. Everything from that point on became uncertain surrounding my career. Under the new ownership it was very likely that the current team of executives would be rearranged. My feelings turned to reality soon after the corporate restructuring took place and I was sent packing with a bruised ego but a hefty severance package in the balance.

In my fall from glory I felt absolutely no pressure to find a new job right away. In the events leading up to the takeover most of my time was monopolized in attempting to save the company. That meant most days and nights I was away from Lisa. So the quality time was welcomed when it was all said and done. It was an opportunity to reacquaint myself with what truly mattered most to me at that time. My love for Lisa! And during my time away from the office I only fell more in love with my wife.

During my time away from the world of high-pressure business numerous recruiting firms who were anxious to place high power executives like me started to make contact. So my resume was circulating across the country to the human resource departments of major financial firms in search of new talent. My previous position as chief financial officer at the upstart telecommunications company raised some important eyebrows along the way. Many companies knew I was available and wagered countless offers to entice my decision to join them. It was a nice position to be in at the time. However, I took my time to research the available positions, the companies and the contracts that were up for grabs. The most lucrative deal came from a company that heavily pursued my skills. It was the powerhouse financial giant, I-Global based out of San Francisco. They originally offered me a deal as a technology analyst that I certainly couldn't refuse. The job outlay was much different from that of calling the shots but I new that at I-Global the future ideas I had would vault me into power and prestige in a hurry. That of course was my primary reason for accepting the position at I-Global. Not to mention the salary and signing bonus they threw at me was one that couldn't be refused.

So after discussing the proposition with Lisa we purchased a loft in downtown San Francisco. Furthermore, Lisa was able to transfer her teaching position to a local junior college. The money was substantially less but she didn't care. She loved teaching and conducting research. The change in geography brought us even closer together at the time. This ultimately proved to be perfect because in our new beginning I also found out that we were expecting our very first child. Lisa announced she was pregnant. I remember the feeling in my heart vividly after hearing her words. I was going to have a baby. Life couldn't have been better.

On the I-Global front I watched the volatility of the complex technology industry. It was definitely my expertise so to speak. At the time it was also a haven for fast cash without considering the long-term and firms the size of I-Global knew exactly that. I-Global was tenacious. I had never been subject to as many meetings until I took the new position. There were daily meetings, weekly meetings, monthly meetings, quarterly meetings, goal-setting meetings, annual meetings, team meetings and executive meetings. You name it there was a meeting that took place. It was insane and so were the demands on my time. It was at this time that I learned firsthand the corporate commandments of I-Global. I learned that your life was secondary to the objectives of the company. If you didn't understand these rules you were 100% expendable. In plain English you had to sell your soul to the corporate devil or else they would see to it that you were out on the street in no time. It was the military of business practices. Understandable to a point because there was always someone else who would die to get their claws on your job. The image of success was a portrait that was all too often painted by the executives at I-Global preaching loyalty and hard work. Success was rewarded publicly within the firm with celebrations to rally the troops. However, failure was not considered an option, carrying heavy consequences. The fear of failure was an urban legend around the halls of I-Global. It was apparent that you had better be sharp 24/7 or else you would be thrown to the hungry lions.

So in order to do it right you had to play by their rules. Meaning you had to become what they wanted you to be. A mold so to speak! A sellout. I found that idea appauling as I watched people one by one become entirely ruthless individuals in front of my very own eyes. On the other hand, for myself, I learned to play the corporate game to get exactly what I wanted. I had images of the title CEO, CFO or COO in mind. The power, money and prestige that accompanied these positions would be mine very soon. I just knew it! After witnessing the daily actions of the so-called power players at I-Global I knew it wouldn't take long to get to the top. I would be giving television interviews, news reports, magazine exclusives and flying around the globe conducting major business deals. I was destined to dine in the finest restaurants in the world, with the most influential business people of our time. I could see the mansion in the suburbs, the expensive cars, the endless flow of money and the finest of everything in my life. I literally saw how all of this was going to play out before it had even started. It made me grin from ear to ear every time I entered the entranceway of I-Global. They had what I wanted. I could not only see it, but I could taste it too. However, to get what I envisioned I would also have to play a very strategic game.

I was not inclined to sell my soul at the time because of my already established principles but that would later change as I gradually got swept into the fast paced dealings at I-Global. Hopefully my vision for the future would stand tall down the road. It had to as I underwent the most profound change in identity in my entire life since meeting Lisa. The selling of my soul I guess you could say at first began with resistance and then became absorbed by the corporate devil. Yes, I too got swept away by the visions of money and power. Beyond my control! Amidst all of the action I definitely could say that I had transformed into someone and something else that I was completely unfamiliar with.

Chapter Three:
The Invitation

"Every moment is a golden one for him who has
the vision to recognize it as such."
-Henry Miller-

My stay at the hospital was lengthening by the weeks. As Dr. Marshall had promised I was moved to a general level suite. Undeniably, it was a tremendous upgrade from the previous prison cell that I inhabited. For starters, the new room had windows that allowed the light to shine through. Finally, access to the outside world! Furthermore, I had a television, radio and telephone all at my fingertips. The very first thing I accomplished in my new place of residence was to get caught up with the happenings in the business world that I so abruptly left behind. I was quite eager to make up for what I'd missed. So I did. Making full usage of the television, newspaper and telephone granted to me. Nothing was going to stop me. Certainly not a little set back like almost killing myself. Back to business I thought. So that is what I started to do. Exactly all that I knew!

As my hospital visit continued I was subjected to countless tests and procedures. Dr. Marshall was adamant about overhauling my body to make sure that physically I was of sound health. So nothing was left out. My interpretation was that he thought of me as a junkie. At first, I denied that very observation but the longer my stay the more the withdrawal symptoms began to become regular. At first there was the uncontrollable shaking, the trembling, the profuse sweating, the nausea and even the vomiting. Then it progressed to aggravation, irritation and even depression. The cravings for a fix were nothing but constant. In fact, for a while it was all I thought about. Especially because the longer I was alone with the self that I so deeply despised the more I wanted some mode of escape. Illicit drugs worked in my life many times before so addict or not that is all I knew to accomplish the task. No matter how hard I tried to absorb myself in my work it was the darkness that prevailed inside of me that I believe led me to my obsession with wanting to leave the very world I inhabited.

It was no secret that I was a very sick individual. It was painful to urinate. Tortuous to sleep. Fatiguing to walk. Depressing to eat. Even shameful to live! Not a day went by that I didn't suffer from the symptoms of being drug deprived until Dr. Marshall had enough information from the battery of tests to finally administer some withdrawal related medications to help an addict survive humanly. There I was, one completely desperate soul who nearly ended his life due to substance abuse. All of which I blamed on the turn of events in my life, in the midst of a craving, sweating, shaking and agitated watching the stock market from a hospital bed. My life was at an all time low so I turned to exactly what I knew. If doping myself up with cocaine was inaccessible during my time in the hospital the next best thing to take my mind off the desire to escape life was business. In retrospect, it started to become more obvious that what I really did best was walk away from the problems in my life. It was far easier to blame other parties for the direction I was heading rather than assume any responsibility myself.

"Hello Mr. Jaimeson," said a low mono toned voice.

Robert! I exclaimed. It's so good to finally see a familiar face.

It was Robert Stanwick the CEO of I-Global. The man who was responsible for hiring me to run the tech sector and about as close to any sort of friend I had in this world. I guess that only superceded the fact that I kept padding his wallet with financial growth along the way.

"We weren't to sure what caused your unlikely disappearance Michael," he stated.

Oh, that! I replied.

"It's not like you to go AWOL on us. Are you all right? I am very concerned."

I put on my charming façade contemplating the horrible situation I was about to engage with my boss.

Well, Robert I suppose I owe you one colossal apology?

"Forget about apologies, Michael. I want some answers," he replied.

I have been in a little bit of a hangover for the past several days. Sorry about that. There is absolutely no excuse for my behavior Robert.

"Listen Michael, I am just glad to hear that you are alright. I tried to call you at home, on your cellular phone. Everything and anything I tried to get a hold of you. You must have 30 messages or so from the office. We finally heard from Dr. Marshall's staff today regarding your disappearance."

So you already know what happened to me?

"Yes, I know most of the story. Its not a pretty thing you know Michael," he replied.

Look Robert! Spare me the sympathy and help get me out of here would you? All I can think about is what is happening with my fund! Who is running that at the moment? How has it been doing over the past little while? Can't you see I have to get out of this place?

The look on Roberts face said it all.

"Michael, if you could see what I see you would be looking at a very sick man who needs some time to heal."

I can heal back at the office! Being trapped here is only making me worse, I shouted in frustration.

"Your doctor just got through explaining everything to me. You nearly killed yourself with an overdose of cocaine, Michael. Doesn't that scare you at all?"

What it means Robert is that I do my job very well! Part of being on top of the world means maintaining an edge over my fellow competitors. And that is exactly what I have been doing to get the job done!

"Using drugs is not going to get you further ahead, Michael."

Robert had me extremely wound up.

Just mind your own business Robert!

"Surely to god you can see that while your sitting here in a bloody hospital."

Please get me out of here, Robert, I pleaded in desperation.

"Look at you! Your white as a ghost! You've lost a ton of weight. You're agitated. Quite frankly your desperate!"

Please, Robert don't take my life away! I shouted.

"Take your life away!"

Yes! You're all I have right now.

Robert shook his head in disbelief. "I don't even know who this Michael Jaimeson is at the moment. I cannot even fathom that you nearly killed yourself with a serious drug problem and you want to come back to run a division of my company. You are sick, Michael! You have a very serious problem! Something that you have chosen to ignore! Something that I refuse to ignore!"

I do not have a problem, I shouted in my defense.

"The doctor mentioned you were in denial."

Robert's tone became sympathetic.

"Right now all that matters is that you recover from this set back, Michael."

I have sold my soul for I-Global. Sacrificed my family, my friends and my life to adhere to the one thing that matters the most, I yelled in frustration.

"Oh! And what's that Michael?"

I sat up in bed pointing directly toward Robert. Your company! I replied.

"Sure, Michael you have no doubt given me more than I could ever have asked for. There is no denying all of your hard work and effort. Your one in a million, Michael! However, I refuse to stand here preaching to you about your health".

So don't! I shouted in anger.

"You want back into the company, Michael?"

You already know that answer!

"Then you're going to have to meet this ultimatum," Robert replied.

You cannot do this to me, Robert! I yelled in rebuttal.

"You are not to step foot into I-Global without some proof to me that you have successfully completed a drug rehabilitation program. At that point if your fit to continue as my colleague you will sign a contract that entitles I-Global to random drug screens to monitor your progress."

That's ridiculous! You have no right to treat me like this! I shouted.

Robert calmly looked into my eyes. "How does that sound, Michael?"

It's an outrage, I responded sharply to his suggestion. I'll see you at your rival company, I said. I will see to it that I destroy I-Global if it's the last thing I do!

Robert did not at all show any sign of fear.

"You may not see it yet, Michael. You have a promising future ahead of you. You just have to open your eyes to see it. Your not the Michael Jamieson that I know."

Than who am I? I screamed.

"Someone I want to see get better. I cannot let you come back to continue your path of self- destruction. If I do it will only infectiously spread to the people around you and potentially topple the business. That is one responsibility that I do not want to be liable for, Michael. Surely, you can understand?"

You have no right to play god with my life, Robert.

"I am the furthest thing from god, Michael. But you don't have to be god to know when a friend is in trouble. The shattered pieces of your life can still be saved."

Like a caged lion I roared back. Robert never refer to me as your friend! Because this is not how friends treat each other.

43

Robert looked rather torn about our discussion. "Do yourself a favor while you still can, Michael. Take Dr. Marshall's advice. Get some help before it's too late!"

There is nothing quite like kicking a person while they are down! I squealed at Robert.

He just looked at me with a blank stare. "I won't respond to that! You are not the Michael that I know. When you see him though, tell him that his friend Robert misses him. I have to go. My door is always open for you. But please come back healthy. I'll check in with you soon. Take care, Michael."

It was in that moment that Robert turned and disappeared through the doorway of my room. Once again, I was left to contemplate the direction my life was heading. It was surreal to reflect on my visit with Robert. It was as if he were correct in saying that I was not the Michael he knew. Even I knew that long before arriving at the hospital! During the course of our discussion it was as if I was observing the dialogue that took place as a third party. Perhaps he was right. Maybe someone else was in this body called 'Michael'. Robert knew I was in a volatile state. He was there to bear witness to the events leading to the separation of my marriage, the ruthless businessman I had become and the excessive partygoer I played. It never seemed to concern him before. My life that is! So I couldn't help but wonder why it was such a big deal now?

Robert always new I was one to rise to a challenge. It was motivation, met head on the moment that someone told me there was something that couldn't be done. However, taking my job away meant weakening my soul even further. After all, one by one the important sectors of my life began to crumble. It was the clichéd "clean sweep" so to speak. My wife. My daughter. My health. My career. My life. Everything came crashing down. And yet there I was, a completely disillusioned excuse for a human being, sitting, shaking and twitching angrily after being dealt a sorry blow. It was easiest once again to blame someone other than myself for the events that unfolded. I couldn't help but get angry but I was also too physically weak to through the tantrum I could see myself executing in my mind. Instead, my emotions overcame me. In the escalating tension I finally broke down. I lost any composure I had left. I could somehow see bits and pieces of reality during my time of reflection. However, I remained steadfast in my resistance to fully admit that someone other than myself was right.

I must have wept for hours it seemed. During this time I repeatedly reiterated the question "Why me?" I wondered if things could ever change? It was also at that point that I can honestly remember wishing that my life had ended. At that very moment I believed death was the only viable solution to end the downward spiral that my life was experiencing. I wished for the entire nightmare to just end somehow. During that time I wanted to escape. To run free from the darkness! I felt the urge for a fix growing inside. A way to ease the harsh reality that was settling in to my life! For me a drug's high was a sanctuary to hide in recluse for a while.

"Well Michael, I can see this has been a rather rough morning for you," said a voice.

It was Dr. Marshall that spoke to me from the hallway outside my room.

What do you mean by that? I replied.

"The obvious signs of drug withdrawal have entered the picture, I can see."

Oh that! I remarked. No I am just experiencing some pain at the moment.

"Real Pain? Dr. Marshall asked.

Real Pain!

"Describe it for me Michael."

I winced in discomfort and pointed. It's a generalized stiffness that is all over. Quite excruciating, Dr. Marshall. Isn't there anything you can give me for that?

Dr. Marshall mustered a smile. "Ah the confessions of a drug addict. Nice try, Michael."

No I am 100% serious about this, I rebutted in frustration.

"I am sure you are, but the effects of withdrawal can be horrific. After all, your true sickness, your dependence is expressing itself throughout your body. You're fighting."

As my eyes watered up, my voice began to crack as I told Dr. Marshall that my fight was over.

I am far too tired to defend myself any longer. God should have ended my disastrous life when he had one foot in the coffin but he refused. Instead I am alive but my life is over! I have nothing that is honestly worth living for.

Dr. Marshall approached my bed taking a seat at the foot of it. "I don't know you all that well Michael. But I do understand that you are married with a daughter, correct?"

Yes, I am separated from both my wife and daughter at present.

"What about your career?" he asked.

It's apparently over until I get my life back on track.

"How about your friends?"

In my line of work you tend to burn every bridge you have to ensure your success. Personal connections are simply a distraction because they leave you vulnerable to the others waiting for your failure.

"What of your family?"

I haven't spoken to my mother or father since my wedding. There was far too much personal drama I suppose. They are very controlling people and the meddling in our lives took a toll. You cannot treat an adult as if he were a child.

Dr. Marshall's usual cheer diminished to a soft, sympathetic voice. "You know Michael I don't really know what to say. I guess things are looking pretty dark for you right now!"

You can say that again, Dr. Marshall, I replied without any argument whatsoever.

"So what do you plan on doing?" he asked me.

I am really not sure, I said.

"That self pity of yours could surely use a pick me up I'll bet," he stated abruptly.

Don't start messing with my head, Dr. Marshall.

"No games here, Michael. It's just that I came to tell you that you should consider yourself lucky."

How could my life be in any way lucky? I asked.

"The results of all your physical tests have rendered your systems function to be within normal limits. In fact, your body is all set to go back to the punishing that I assume you'll be continuing in the very near future."

Does that mean I am free to go? I asked.

"I suppose it does mean that you are at least physically ready to resume your life. However, keep in mind that you are undergoing some serious effects of withdrawal that would be better suited to medical care under a supervised rehabilitation program."

Rehabilitation is something that I can do on my own.

"Well, that is your choice, Michael. However, I would professionally advise you to check-in routinely with me to monitor your medications and recovery."

Dr. Marshall I am not sure you heard me correctly. I have no friends! No family! No job! Nothing! The only thing I need right now is a little disappearing act to leave the darkness that has been cast on my life.

Dr. Marshall's face went blank. "Michael, you have other options."

Well, I guess I see it differently than you, I replied bluntly.

"It is apparent that on the larger scale you have your health. However, drug addiction is a sickness that you have to deal with. Not only that, you have a whole host of mental healing that obviously needs to be accomplished."

As I mentioned before, I am not at all interested in your help.

Dr. Marshall took an upbeat response. "You can overcome your past tragedies and turn them into triumphs. I have seen examples of it thousands of times, Michael."

Really! I replied sarcastically in thought of his comments.

"You think you are the only one on this planet who has ever endured hardships in their life, Michael?"

No! But I'll bet that most have never sunk as low as my life has! I argued.

"Michael, once you get over your huge ego perhaps you'll see that there is a whole world out there that exists around you. I believe the chip on your shoulder is so big at this point that your narcissism has interfered with your cognition of what life is truly about. In fact, I have a diagnosis for that."

So what does that entail? I fought back intently.

I was dying to hear Dr. Marshall's keen insight.

Dr. Marshall appeared to be fighting a smile. "It's called Cerebral Constipation."

There was no way I could keep a straight face in response to Dr. Marshall's diagnosis. So I burst out laughing in hysterics along with him. In all I believe Dr. Marshall accomplished something albeit I could not put my finger on his strategy. However, I could sense a difference in my persona despite his efforts.

After we laughed at the diagnosis Dr. Marshall quickly picked up where he left off.

"In all seriousness, Michael, there are many more reasons to live than die. It's far too easy to give up when things get rough. The world is an exquisite place to live! Especially, if you haven't truly seen it before! Maybe you should stick around awhile and see what I am talking about?"

Despite my effort to resist I was blown away by the final comments of Dr. Marshall. And I couldn't help but wonder what he had meant by talking about truly seeing the world we live in.

Maybe I'll give it some thought, I replied.

"Please think about it Michael!" He said. "You will be so happy you did. Oh and one more thing Mr. Jaimeson. This afternoon I will be driving out to the Monterey Peninsula to visit a friend of mine. Someone I would very much like you to meet. Why don't you join me?"

Assuming a comedic performance I said. Look Doc, I am definitely a little desperate as you can see but not that desperate. Dr. Marshall was laughing.

"Well, I am certainly glad to see you haven't lost your sense of humor, Michael."

So you're not asking me on a date?

"No, I want you to accompany me to a world class rehabilitation center that is run by a friend of mine."

Oh, I see what your up to. No bloody way, I yelled in resistance.

"Its not what you think, Michael. Trust me on this when I say this is not like the rehab centers you see in the movies."

Why should I trust you, Dr. Marshall?

"Simply because you have nothing else to lose right now."

I suppose to some degree you are right! I have nothing to lose because everything in my life is already gone.

Dr. Marshall quickly dodged the self-attack I commenced.

"The facility we will be visiting is frequented by people from all over the world because of its new age system dealing with the art of personal development. Everyone from movie stars, professional athletes, politicians and corporate moguls like yourself travel there for help."

You honestly think I need help at this point?

"It would be an absolutely life changing experience, Michael. And right now it looks as though you could use one."

I'll think about it, Dr. Marshall.

"Great, I'll take that as a yes, Michael. I will let them know to expect our arrival. Pick you up at three o'clock this afternoon. You won't be sorry with your decision," Dr. Marshall stated in his usual bright cheery voice.

I didn't say I would be going with you, I exclaimed quite abrasively.

"No, but I can see the answer in your eyes, Michael."

Really?

"Yes, you're not that different from anyone else on this planet."

How so?

"You have been searching your entire life for answers. Something you've been hoping to find to fill the sense of void in your life."

You feel pretty confident about that, don't you?

"I have seen it a thousand times! The invitation I extended to you has been accepted. See you at three, Michael."

Then Dr. Marshall vanished from my room leaving me to swim in the "puddle of mud" that was my life. No one cared about me. I had no where to turn. No one to separate me from myself, until the invitation appeared by Dr. Marshall! The crazy conniving shrink had done it. In all of my time alone I labored endlessly in punishing myself for everything I had done up to that point in my life. Dr. Marshall indirectly severed that connection long enough to get me to listen to someone other than myself. Dr. Marshall successfully broke my descent into self-pity for a few short moments. A time that was long enough for my already full-grown ego to see beyond itself. Several minutes in fact where I didn't even think about me! Instead, listening closely to the passion that existed in his voice for life. Something had definitely intrigued me enough to forget about my own personal drama for the time being. Whatever it was it had worked.

After some thought, I admitted to myself that Dr. Marshall was correct in saying that I had nothing to lose by traveling with him to visit with his friend. To a greater extent I wanted to find out more. I wanted to know what he knew about life. More so, the answers he saw when he looked into my eyes. Obviously, I had a great deal to learn. Since I was starting fresh, what could it hurt? At worst it would be a method to salvage my life back free of toxic drugs. Once I could chemically flush the need to escape the world I might perhaps be able to return to my career in the corporate dungeon. It was my only hope. And maybe that is what Dr. Marshall was attempting to accomplish with his little pep talk. Establish some hope in a person that definitely had none. If worse came to worse I could leave. I was free to go. I clearly understood my options. So I made a mental note to be open-minded about the experience I was about to embark upon. The sales job I did must have worked because despite all of my egoic resistance I did leave the hospital that day a weakened soul in search of something more. Dr. Marshall convinced me that an alternative to the darkness I was experiencing did exist. In desperate need of answers and even more so direction I began the next leg of my journey that very day with Dr. Marshall's invitation.

Reflection

"An integral being knows without going,
sees without looking and accepts without doing."
-Lao Tzu-

Six months after entering the world of I-Global as an analyst I inked a deal that sold my soul to the company. Of course it was my own doing. Fueled by none other than my naive passion and hunger for wealth. I wanted success to rain down on my life. To some extent I was already very much a success. A 32-year old sought after executive that was advising I-Global traders to buy and sell stocks based on my tutelage. In doing so amidst the technology explosion the company made a fortune. Not only did I pad their portfolio but I ensured their future as well.

You see I saw the tech plummet approaching. So any investments I studied were completed to make a quick buck and then we pulled clear. However, I grew extremely bored with the analyst role I was involved in. So I developed a strategy I had been thinking about for quite some time. Knowing that I was the proverbial "Prince of Babylon" at that time I approached I-Global CEO Robert Stanwick with a visionary look to the future. It was an idea that had been locked in my head for years. A creation that was revolutionary in design with the purpose to place I-Global on the information technology map.

I pitched the idea to Stanwick over lunch. The vision was to create a technology fund sector within the company that would include various investor risk ratios. One of the funds would include the less riskier prominent tech companies that would consistently earn growth over the long-term. The other funds would include moderate to high-risk companies on the market. Certainly, a little more dangerous but extremely lucrative if watched closely. At the time I-Global was a company synonymous with investors around the globe. Branching the companies horizons was always something to be considered. However, the idea was revolutionary. I had it researched in fine detail. The map was in place. All I needed was the go ahead to make it all real.

Robert was as enthused as I had ever seen him with my sales pitch. In fact, so much that he summoned an emergency board of directors meeting so I could present the proposal to the ultimate decision makers. Robert understood that the plan was my "baby" so to speak. I wanted to make it clear that I was to head up the command post for the fund sector. He laughed when I made the idea evident. Telling me that I would be the fund manager instead of what I assumed

EIGHT DAYS IN MAY

would be an analyst position. Something told me that Robert had already been doing some thinking of his own in the same arena as I had done. Perhaps the same ideologies as mine to map the future of I-Global.

It was no secret that I-Global was the talk of the financial world for the last several decades. And this is what the company wanted to maintain for the remaining years to come. So my vision became a reality in what seemed to be no time at all. In an instant my thoughts came to fruition as three of the best technology analysts were hired to fall under my guidance to pursue considerable reward in the tech sector. With my ideas in place, Robert was prepared to offer us the monumental task of establishing a number of mutual funds within the tech market. A risk that perhaps carried a heavy reward! For me, it was a no-brain concept and I could see that the board of directors knew it. My future looked incredibly bright as I went to work with my team to create several of the largest, most lucrative mutual funds that the financial world had ever seen. They took a chance on me by sacrificing their previous sector growth. A tremendously bold statement! I recognized and appreciated the opportunity. It was my stepping-stone to greatness.

As the fund components were mapped out and the game plans were executed my dream became very much a reality. However, it was now up to the companies marketing department to sell the infantile funds to new and existing investors. At the time the tech sector was powerful. In fact, everyone wanted in because it was making a killing. So the funds naturally became a hit all on their own. Robert wanted me to sit back assuming a more passive role in managing the funds. But my instinct was to have incredible diversity within each one.

To make that successful I hired lead fund managers whose strengths revolved around the spectrum of the companies comprising the funds. Since my area of expertise was technology I had no problem managing but I wanted to be hands-on. In fact, I wanted to head the high-risk fund in the portfolio. So I did. Of course it was also the most volatile area to become involved with but the excitement that accompanied the risky dealings fueled my drive for success. Essentially, it was the birth of my career and the death of my life. Managing funds of this nature certainly meant earning more money but it also carried a heavy burden on my timetable.

The city of San Francisco during the height of the infamous tech boom was an explosively expensive place to live. So, the more money we had the better off we would be especially following the birth of the baby. Lisa in preparation for the arrival had taken a leave of absence from her teaching position. However, the more money you made at I-Global the more the demands on your time evolved. Not only were the hours grueling but so too was the added pressure I had to face on a daily basis. The day's events encompassed my being glued to countless computer screens and attached to numerous phone lines. When the markets moved we had to be ready to attack. What was even worse was my extensive history of being a control freak. That meant I had a hand in everything morning, noon and night.

When the markets closed at days end I was able to leave the battleground to debrief the upper echelon of executives in the early evening. Following these seemingly endless discussions there wasn't much time left for my wife Lisa. There were also many occasions where I was summoned to fly around the globe for weeks on end to get business deals completed. It was all about business. I became all about business. All of which placed a great deal of strain on my marriage.

I was convinced I could somehow balance the best of both worlds. However, to my amazement the fund I managed grew to unbelievable proportions. During that time everyone under the sun wanted to monopolize my efforts. The growth was precedent setting. It hit record numbers in its sector making it a very hot commodity for investors looking for a cash grab. In no time millions upon millions of dollars were pouring into the I-Global accounts. The penthouse crew at the executive level began to see a prodigy in the making and started to take notice. I was wined, dined and heavily rewarded for my instant success. Lisa on the other hand witnessed the arrival of a star and the departure of the husband she use to know.

The deeper my accomplishments became, the larger the rewards that accompanied them. I was a millionaire at the age of thirty-two. My face was plastered all over the front pages of industry magazines. I was the talk of the town. A regular on financial news programs and the highlight of many private interviews! I was in constant demand but I never once left my post at the battlefield. This placed an even surmounting tension on my already insane schedule. However, I adored the limelight. In fact, I was such a television regular that Lisa would often joke that she would spend more time with me on television than in real life. It didn't take me long to see the content of those remarks were passive-aggressive. It was a tense topic, my career path that is. However, a subject I motioned to avoid whenever I could. Once again doing what I did best. Evading the problem.

In understanding Lisa's feelings regarding my time away we began to release those pressures by placing our energies into shopping the market for a new home. It was the search for Lisa's dream house. It was a bustling project that I decided to be as much a part of as I could. However, visiting million dollar mansions in the suburbs of San Francisco was a daunting task. After the initial frustration had passed Lisa settled on a "fix me up" 10,000 square foot monster of a home. The work would take months. The detail and décor even longer! However, my wife had a vision and I encouraged her to follow her heart. She worked very passionately on the home with every ounce of her soul until the seemingly endless task was completed. The home was remarkable. A creation from the depths of Lisa imagination! During the renovation period the tension in our relationship was diverted. It wasn't even a topic of conversation as she became so enthralled in her destiny to make her dream come true.

Upon completion the stunning estate was ready for our arrival and that too of our beautiful baby daughter. Eva was born into the world without complication, arriving home the day after her birth. Between the house and the baby I reached a safety net of freedom from the pressures of my hectic schedule. I even solidified my position by helping Lisa to hire a nanny to relieve some of the burden of motherhood. However, I was only riding out a very short wave. It was clearly temporary, as the pressures at home would once again escalate.

There wasn't a doubt in my mind that with my new daughter a part of me wanted to be at home. However, I succumbed to the demands of my career. In fact, I let them consume me. I had responsibility after responsibility thrown in my face every waking hour in the workplace. But Lisa just couldn't understand. I hired people to look after the yard, the general maintenance, the housekeeping and even the baby. I even showered Lisa with lavish gifts to help ease the burden of my being absent from her life. In fact, together we purchased one of the most incredible little beach houses you could find on the Monterey Bay. A place that Lisa and I treasured so much. The place we would escape to fall in love all over again. It was a magical place for us in the past.

However, none of the purchases substituted for what Lisa desired most. And that was to have me back in her life. The arguments were often. The words increasingly harsh! The emotions raged out of control. Lisa grew to hate my career as my lust for greatness became increasingly reinforced. Not a day went by where I didn't hear that I loved my job more than I did my family. It was at that time that I even started to take ownership in her words. In fact, I not only agreed with her. I believed it myself. You see, I didn't have any sense of personal identity with just being a husband or a father. It was my ascent towards the heights of success that provided my life with the importance that I longed to have.

So the pressures from my wife began to tug at my inner self, what at least remained of it. However, what remained of my soul belonged to I-Global. So with my collapsing marriage, the demands of being a fund manager and my aspirations to reach the heavens it all hit me like a freight train. My life grew to become unbearable. It was simply too much. And I was having trouble with finding a place to run and hide. So I embarked on the next best thing to find temporary security. I detached from it. It was at that juncture in my life that I turned to drugs and alcohol as a mechanism for escape. My way out! It was an activity that was initiated sparingly but managed to pick up immense steam as the pressures mounted. The greater the demands, the more I frequented the numbness that these elements provided. Pretty soon I carried my own stash. Yes, I had the paraphernalia that indicated I was a full fledged drug abuser. Whether it was at work, home, driving, flying I began to constantly beckon my call to leave behind my crumbling life. It seemed as though I had lost control of my direction during that time. And I did. There you have it. The confessions of a fallen man in the making.

Chapter Four:
Gut Check Time

"You can't have a better tomorrow if your thinking
about yesterday all of the time."
-Charles F. Kettering-

When I envisioned a drug rehabilitation facility the picture in my mind detailed something related to a low security prison. Images of security guards surrounding the structure were vivid. A heavily guarded entranceway protected by barbed wire also came to the forefront. However, as Dr. Marshall and I pulled into the entryway of the center I had to admit that I was pleasantly surprised. The center looked like something out of a travel magazine. A resort nestled into the Cliffside overlooking the Pacific Ocean. No guards. No criminals. No hatred. Just people longing to find the hope of a new tomorrow.

As Dr. Marshall and I entered the lobby the doorman greeted us with great pizzazz. After shaking hands he welcomed us to the center by directing us to the guest services counter. Upon my entry he asked to take my luggage albeit very limited. As he attended to my bag in my perplexity over the entire situation I could see Dr. Marshall scouting the magnificent lobby for his friend Tom.

During the process of our arrival Dr. Marshall led me toward what appeared to be a check-in desk.

"Michael, come over here and meet Louisa the head of guest services here at the center. She is going to get you situated. Louisa, this is my friend Michael. He is going to be staying with you for the next little while."

I enjoyed the introduction made by Dr. Marshall as I shook the hand of a short, stout, Native American woman standing behind the reception area.

It is very nice to meet you! This is quite a place. I said to break the ice.

"Sort of Mr. Jamieson."

What do you mean?

"The only difference with the center is that the people who stay here with us never come back."

It sounded very eerie to hear that response while surrounded by the beauty of the center.

"Here is your room key Mr. Jamieson. Room number 410 is overlooking the ocean. You'll understand what I mean by never having to return very soon sir."

So how does this whole operation work? I asked Louisa.

But before she had time to respond to my eager question I felt the presence of an inexplicit energy, just over my right shoulder. As I turned around I could see Dr. Marshall standing next to an athletic looking, forty-something man dressed in a Hawaiian shirt, shorts and wearing flip-flops.

"You must be the infamous Michael Jamieson," said the surf dude in front of me.

And you are?

"My name is Tom. Welcome to the center," he stated with great enthusiasm.

Thank you!

"It is a real pleasure to meet someone that Dr. Marshall thinks so highly of."

Tom motioned to Louisa that he would be handling everything from here on out.

"I'll give you the run down on how this facility works, Michael. Are you ready for the grand tour?" He shouted with vigor.

About as ready as I am going to be, I suppose.

"Great! Lets get started shall we?"

So Tom, Dr. Marshall and I left the lobby heading down the west corridor of the center. On our walk the building appeared nothing like I imagined. There were beautiful flowers, trees and vegetation growing within its confines. The halls were magnificent with towering cathedral ceilings and large open windows looking outside. The corridor was lined with large panes of glass that enabled abundant rays of sunlight to enter the inside. Through the glass on our journey I could see exquisite courtyards furnished with waterfalls, trickling streams and colorful floral arrangements. Cozy chairs and tables occupied the scene lending to its serenity.

As we continued the tour Tom pointed out the main cafeteria where all the major meals would be served. He also mentioned that the food was all 100% organic in nature to aid with the healing process of the body. There was 24-hour access to food either by visiting the cafeteria or through the use of room service. The choices included buffet or menu items. Next we passed by a half dozen conference rooms where many people seemed to be engaged in discussion behind closed doors. Tom indicated that these were where all drug counseling sessions took place. We furthered the walk to arrive at a laboratory used to process blood and urine of the registered guests at the center. The testing would take place on random occasions and an on-site medical doctor would oversee the direction. Tom also mentioned that the medical staff was available to tend to every need of the guests during their recovery process. The lab was the first stop on my leg through the west corridor as it was indicated that they required a blood and urine sample before initiating the program.

"Michael," Tom said. "Dr. Marshall and I are going to leave you in the hands of the lab staff for about fifteen minutes or so. At this time they are going to get base samples of your blood and urine. Over the course of the next month or so you will be required to give random samples as requested by the staff at the lab. These are great people. So you have nothing to worry about. See you in fifteen minutes, Michael," Tom shouted as he and Dr. Marshall continued down the west corridor.

It was at that very moment that my true physical self decided to enter the picture. Amazed by all the preceding events I had forgotten that I was indeed a recovering drug addict. I felt a large grumble from the deep confines of my stomach as the nervousness of not being able to control the process overcame my body. Despite the agitation, shaking and weakness I was experiencing I wasn't sure if the nervousness was part of the withdrawal or whether it meant that it was "gut check time." I had always feared the unknowns because I simply could not control them. It was certainly a vast ocean of unknowns. The whole process of subjecting myself to drug rehabilitation was fearful for me. I am pretty certain it was "gut check time."

Despite my anxiety over the entire process of detoxifying myself I committed to the process. In fact, I had no other choice to at least get my career back on the right track. Furthermore, I was far too tired to battle the inclinations of Dr. Marshall. Once I sacrificed my bodily fluids I knew I was starting a new chapter in my life. After the samples were retrieved I started back down the west corridor to find Dr. Marshall and Tom. Upon reuniting with the two I remember feeling overly weak. After being exposed like a lab rat I became light-headed and feverish. Suddenly experiencing nausea and the urge to vomit.

Uncontrollably, I ended up puking at the feet of Dr. Marshall and Tom in the middle of the hallway. To shed some light on the matter Tom was overcome with a shining smile.

"It happens around here all of the time, Mr. Jamieson. Get use to it."

While feeling embarrassed over my actions I did manage to muster a smile to match those of Tom and Dr.Marshall.

"Come on, Michael, there is much more to see," Tom mentioned.

So off we went on the continuation of our trip. I couldn't help but think that Tom was some kind of "oddball". He even seemed a little crazy himself. Could he not see that I needed a bed and a garbage pale to throw up in?

Instead we went on to visit the counseling rooms, lecture halls and photo lab.

"Have a seat Michael," Tom cheerfully stated.

What are we doing I asked?

"We need a picture for your identification card."

Do I have to smile?

"Say cheese," He responded as he snapped a picture of my decrepit face for my pass. "You will look at that picture when you leave and won't even recognize who it is, Michael."

I can hardly wait for that day.

We continued on to visit a large state of the art movie theatre and a fully equipped games room with pool tables and ping-pong. Next was a full service fitness facility and wellness center. There were dumbbells, machines and equipment galore. On the outskirts of the fitness room perimeter were the offices of a naturopathic doctor, massage therapist and doctor of chiropractic. Tom quickly mentioned that the program is highly integrated with the use of all practitioners to deal with the health of every distinct guest. The spa was equipped to provide manicures, pedicures, facials and peels. You name it they had it. Around the corner was a giant resort sized swimming pool resting behind a glass door. It was isolated in a manner to give it maximum sun exposure with the perfect backdrop of volcanic rock, swarmed with eloquent vines. The outdoor area consisted of a large waterfall emptying into a huge in-ground hot tub.

Back in the halls were the office suites of a nutritional counselor, fitness trainers, a physiotherapist, psychologist and psychiatrist. Just down the hall we stopped to see the in-house café, the library and internet kiosk. Next to that was the visitor's lounge where guests could visit with friends, family and loved ones at anytime during their stay. The room was full of comfortable furniture, phones and televisions for an enjoyable, laidback environment.

"The door you see here is a private entrance for the guests, Michael," Tom said as he pointed to what appeared to be a back alley door.

Who would need that?

"People who wish to have privacy without security personnel onsite. It does have a surveillance camera for 24-hour watch but it is kind of nice to keep it as close to home as possible."

All over the center there were security staff for the protection of the guests. Tom explained that in the setting many people are suicidal, self abused, physically abused and seeking a safe haven from the dangerous world of drugs. He furthered his explanation by mentioning that during your stay at the center we were not permitted to leave the premises without security clearance, staff escort or family accompaniment. The only other reason to leave would be a major emergency. There was no access to cars. The only phone and television access was in the guest lounge. And nothing was private when it came to that.

It was my belief that Tom could see I was weakening by the moment as he continued the tour. He explained that my room, 410, was at the end of the East corridor overlooking his favorite view of all. The ocean.

"In your room you will find your clothes and belongings which have passed through a security check. You will also find pajamas and a robe that we supply for your needs. An itinerary of your stay here at the center is posted with times and locations for you to review. You are expected to arrive on time for all of your meetings. This is a paradise that I have created to help heal the many wounded souls that pass through our doors, Michael. Let the healing begin," Tom said in a very serious tone.

This entire center is all accessible to me?

"Everything you see is yours to enjoy during your visit."

After that Tom directed me on the path to arrive at my room.

"One more thing Michael before you head to your room."

Tom proceeded to point through an open window that facilitated a warm breeze in the direction of the ocean.

"You have access at all times, outside of your scheduled hours, to the beach down there. A divine place to reflect as you will find yourself doing a lot of during your stay".

Great! I said in a near death tone.

As I stood with a stooped posture, almost ready to collapse in fatigue I shook the hand of Dr. Marshall one last time as I headed in the direction of my room. While ascending the stairs I thought about the lunatic Tom who ran the joint and what kind of journey I had gotten myself into. I was beginning to second-guess myself at the time. Having extreme doubts. It would not be long until the amazing man of darkness, Michael Jamieson, would cast a cloud upon the beauty of the center he checked into.

As I lethargically stumbled to the last step arriving to room 410 I found myself drenched in a cold sweat. I was suddenly overcome with a sense of dizziness. Upon opening the door to my room I was met with the radiant light that perforated through the rectangular bay window overlooking the ocean. In my opinion the light of the day drowned out the darkness of myself at least for the moment. In reaching this conclusion I met the light with the sudden urge to vomit. Luckily, I made it to a garbage pale nearby. I was ill in countless ways. In fact, both mentally and physically! However, I doubted my readiness for the next stage of recovery. My stomach trembled yet again as I regurgitated my insides fighting back the urge to be sick.

When the initial feelings of illness subsided I was able to take notice of the upcoming schedule posted at my desk. It was detailed down to the last minute from start to finish. The only thing that wasn't booked as far as I could see was the washroom breaks. The frightening thing was that it all began today with a visit from the resident physician who would be conducting a brief physical examination at five o'clock.

My stomach sensations once again initiated a churning as I raced towards the toilet in expectation of more sickness. However, this time it was different in the sense that it was more a nervous reaction. I was right before in my synopsis. Perhaps it was "gut check time." In that instance I collapsed in exhaustion on the bed. But I wasn't out for long until I was rudely interrupted by an annoying buzzing sound that seemed to be coming from a speaker system within my room.

"Mr. Jamieson, this is guest service's on the line. I hope all is well with your room. I just wanted to remind you that your doctor's exam is to be conducted at five o'clock sharp today. Dr. Quantril the staff physician is on his way up to see you."

It was an intercom system that so abruptly disturbed my potential slumber and helped reinstate the violent tremors in my gut that had previously subsided. I couldn't help but think what had I gotten myself into?

Reflection

"You can't do anything about the length of your life,
but you can do something about its width and depth."
-Shira Tehrani-

I will never forget a past Valentine's Day. It was indeed February 14th and the halls of I-Global were abuzz with the energy from a five million dollar profit that my fund had made in a risky venture on the foreign exchange market. The vibe was definitely incredible as we celebrated the victory at the days end. I guess it was fair to say that love was in the air and I was in my element yet again. The booze was a flowing as tomorrow's strategy was discussed.

It was approximately 10 p.m. that evening when I finally arrived home, empty handed, in a drunken stupor to see something that could have only hurt my wife. Lisa in the theme of Valentine's Day had set a place setting for two, highlighted with fancy candles and accented with rose petals. It was very romantic. And it was definitely meant for Lisa and I to rekindle our love for each other.

I remember my grimace of frustration as I felt like a heel for not remembering the event. So very stealth like I proceeded to check in on the baby while not waking Lisa who was asleep. That was all I could recall before passing out on the dressing room chair in the walk-in closet.

The next day my watch alarm woke me only to be met with a pounding headache and an angry wife who was standing by my side. Lisa lit the sky with a fury of comments regarding my behavior. The insults came later. It was Lisa that did all the talking as I readied myself for the working day. After all her synopsis was correct. I simply had no line of defense. So there was no point in fueling her disappointment with my petty words.

It was as if I didn't even care about anyone other than myself. I knew it had to be because I couldn't stand the thought of looking into Lisa's eyes during her scathing attack. I was emotionally detached. Numb where my home life was concerned. Lisa and the baby were not my top priority. Lisa clearly witnessed that. However, at that point I started to take notice of what that was doing to our relationship.

I remember telling Lisa that I didn't have time for the banter as I had to get to work. My career was always the way out of any serious discussion that I wanted to avoid. On my way to the car Lisa's last words rattled my cage. She mentioned that ever since I joined with I-Global that I wasn't the same Michael that she had fallen in love with. Hearing those words reinforced the cold, egotistical, maniac I was evolving to be. My response was silence. I refrained from yelling. Again, she had every right to express her frustrations regarding me. However, I did change. I saw the initiation but failed to accept the reality. The change wasn't for my wife or family. It was for me and she knew it. I think in that moment it was my acceptance of the fact that I had already left my marriage behind.

So I walked down the hallway to a key rack on the wall. I took two keys and threw them down on the kitchen counter. After turning to Lisa, I asked her which key she wanted to take. She was perplexed by my actions. You see the two keys were for our house in San Francisco and the beach house in Monterey. I told her that I didn't want her to continue living in pain from what I was doing. After apologizing for my life direction I asked Lisa where she and the baby wanted to live. Her jaw dropped in dismay. She was absolutely blown away by my decision to give up on our marriage.

Many minutes of silence had passed. Again, I posed the question of where she preferred to live. It was then that I saw the tears stream from the beautiful eyes that caught my heart so many years ago. She didn't want to give up. In fact, Lisa pleaded with me to change my mind. She suggested counseling. Something I would never agree to because of time constraints. Lisa mentioned a vacation together. Again, a shot at the stars because work commanded my every move! She only wanted me. My love to be returned for that which she offered me. However, I couldn't give her what she wanted at that time. I wasn't sure if I could ever provide her with the love she deserved. I was far too wound up in my own personal storm of emotions to be around someone as precious as my wife.

So I proposed the solution of time away from each other to reflect on our future. It was not the topic that Lisa had wanted to hear. She was visibly distraught. Her emotions were on the table. However, I felt nothing. In fact, at that time I was hollow inside. I felt overcome with emptiness. Lisa had questions. Questions that I neither had the time nor the patience to answer. There was no other woman. No need to stray. Actually, no time to think of anything other than business!

I remembered looking at the beautiful individual I grew to know and felt no loss of love. Selling my life to my own ego dependent aspirations subjected Lisa to a life of being alone. In her loneliness I kept her at a distance from my hunger to be the "Corporate King of Camelot." She had no clue what it was that I wanted in life because I never communicated my dreams to the woman I loved. I left her in the dark. And I am not sure why. Perhaps to protect her from the idea that I wanted something far greater than to be a husband and a father! I never communicated my vision to her however I believe she saw the priority in my demeanor.

On February 15th, the day after Valentine's Day I walked out on my wife and daughter. Not only did I leave them out of my path in life. I left them without answers. Since that day there had been no contact. No communication. It all ended as I left them behind to rush off to what I felt at the time was far more important. My identity. The career climb I was making at I-Global.

Lisa had taken the baby and all of their belongings to make residence at the beach house outside of San Francisco. I really couldn't blame her for seeking refuge in such a beautiful backdrop. Since that day I verbally made it clear that I had detached myself from the things that actually matter. In communicating that message I turned my drug use up from a social status to full-time.

Following the days after my separation from Lisa I was never able to sleep at night. No matter how much I drank or how much I snorted the thought of being alone at night with myself became unbearable. I hated what I had become. I despised the things I did to get through a regular day. But in time I accepted my decision. To distance myself from anything that mattered. From anything with personal meaning! All except work of course because my career was my obsession. From that day on I concluded that meaningful people added distractions to the ascent I was making to the top of corporate America. I vowed that nothing was going to stand in my way! Certainly, a promise that I obviously kept with myself.

Chapter Five:
The Journey & the Guide

"What lies behind us and what lies before us
are tiny matters compared to what lies within us."
-Ralph Waldo Emerson-

My original plan of attack upon entering the center was to meet the ultimatum set forth by my boss Robert Stanwick. I knew that if I could become sober I had a chance at getting at least one lost piece of my life back. That was my strategy, not because I wanted a healthier lifestyle, but because it was the only mode of passage I had to shake the restraints of being labeled a wall-street drug addict.

Suddenly, the intercom came to life as it announced that it was time to get ready for the days opening events. I rolled out of bed only to notice that my stomach had stopped its spiraling journey. The shaking and the sweating seemed to also be on hold. I concluded that the medical doctors increased dosage of detoxification medications were beginning to take effect.

The day's outline was posted on my mirror. It was 5 a.m. and I was due to meet with the staff in the fitness center by 5:30 a.m. Depleted of energy and substance all I really wanted to do was sleep. My body was extremely fatigued from the punishment it adhered. I grew increasingly tired with the idea of exercise. I was never one who had time to workout and my uniquely open schedule at present certainly didn't fuel my desire to start.

My overwhelming mindset to return to slumber had won out.

"Screw this," I said out loud to myself. And I jumped back into to bed.

No sooner did I get back to dream land when I heard a knock at my door. When I arose to answer it, I could see that Tom had come to summon me to participate in the 5:30 a.m. workout session.

Tom was smiling ear to ear. "You okay, Michael?" Tom asked when I opened the door.

Yes, I am just really tired, I replied.

"Well, kicking a drug habit will do that to you."

So I have been told.

"Get use to it for the next little while. Right now the plan of action is to get you to the gym. So get dressed and we'll begin to put a dent in that endless physical fatigue your suffering from, Michael."

Squinting from the bright light of the room I managed to create a noticeable frown as I was being forced against my will to get out of bed. Tom was no doubt conscious about his health. He appeared lean, muscular and fit. He obviously made fitness a lifestyle as he stood before me in a tank top, athletic shorts and wearing a pair of spacey looking running shoes.

"What you give your body is also what you get out of your body, Michael," Tom said. "You can expect every morning to be doing something physical to start your day. It is a method to cleanse your body. Release your tension. Build your immunity and strengthen your soul."

Are you serious! I replied with intense dissatisfaction.

"No kidding at all."

Every morning starts this way?

"You will be working with a personal trainer until you become comfortable with your program. It encompasses a balance of cardiovascular training, weight lifting and stretching."

Oh fantastic! I stated with a sarcastic tone.

"You will become addicted to exercise faster than those drugs you were on, Michael. Just you wait and see," Tom stated confidently.

We'll see about that!

"It's a natural high that you will be experiencing instead of the one your use too. When you come to know the true feeling of being alive you will no doubt find it addictive."

And off we went at 5:30 a.m. to use up what tiny bit of fuel I had remaining in my already depleted tank. When we arrived at the fitness center it was teaming with a handful of other lost souls savagely interrupted from their beds.

"Good morning everyone!" A loud deafening voice shouted. It was Tom the "crazy man." Except this time he had a microphone in his hand. He went into a little 5:30 a.m. motivational speech to rally the sleepy eyed drug addicts. However, I wasn't so sure it did any good as everyone including me looked as though they were running on empty.

"Listen, before you get started this morning I just want to welcome you all to the experience that is going to change your life forever. I understand you have all come to the center to help resolve a dangerous addiction. However, it wouldn't be fair to you to focus solely on the physical realm of drug dependency. There are numerous areas of your life that must be treated as a whole system. At the center we intend to show you the road to conquering your weakness. Furthermore, you are about to embark on a journey that will make you open your eyes in amazement to see a high that is far beyond any chemical creation. The high that I am talking about is in relationship to your lives. It is this premise that has placed the center as a world-renowned entity in transforming the lives of thousands of people around the globe each year. I know it all seems very superficial to you at present. But, I assure you that it will all make sense as you begin a new chapter in your journey. That being said, your travels begin this morning where you will learn about the importance of a healthy lifestyle. Something that is termed wellness!"

"You have all made lifestyle decisions that involved drugs, alcohol and cigarettes. Instead of promoting substances that can harm you we are going to show you the ingredients to preserve your life to full capacity. The training staff is about to enlighten you on the topics of exercise, diet and wellness as a strategy to attain and maintain a healthy body."

With the conclusion of Tom's opening words he clapped his hands firmly together. In a repetitive manner he became a one-man applause as he congratulated us all for having enough sense to acknowledge that our lives could change course. Then he shouted at the top of his lungs. "Today is the first day in your new lives. Welcome home!"

There was no doubt that Tom was a little bit odd. However, his opening speech revealed a certain genuine quality that I failed to see during our initial meeting. The pep talk was surprisingly motivating even for 5:30 a.m. when I looked back at it. What interested me even more were Tom's comments regarding our journey here to the center and beyond. I wasn't quite sure what I was involved in. I thought it was rehabilitation for drug and alcohol addiction. However, Tom clearly had a different agenda put in place to heal the cracks in the foundations of our lives.

The program started by dividing us into two small groups. We began by visiting with three personal trainers in a closed office. Each of us was educated with regards to the importance of exercise in general terms. Later we were familiarized with the topics of aerobic training, resistance training, core training and stretching. The trainers were excellent in their presentation as they emphasized the necessity to cleanse the body of harmful toxins. They stressed the importance of building a strong cardiovascular system. The need to decrease mental stress, control weight and increase the longevity of life through the outlet of fitness as a lifestyle. At times I had to roll my eyes. We were clearly worn souls who were being pushed to the capacity by motivated staffers. What would result from putting a drug dependent fragile frame on a treadmill I wondered? I personally couldn't see anyone with enough stamina to last more than two minutes before collapsing.

All criticism aside we got up and moving as we were introduced to the cardio machines that loitered the gym floor. Things like treadmills, stationary bikes, ergometers and stairclimbers. Next, it was the weight equipment. The first day was nothing but introduction. However, it was constantly emphasized that each morning was going to start in the gym at 5:30 a.m. working out. The only exception was Sunday. The only day off we were to have. We would be working closely with the guidance of a personal trainer during that time until we became proficient enough to carry on our own program.

After the tour of the fitness room floor we were off to meet the wellness staff headed by Dr. Smith, a Doctor of Chiropractic. He wanted us to understand that wellness was about the detection, prevention and maintenance of the body before the onset of signs, symptoms and health problems. Dr. Smith joyfully encouraged us in our path to reach this level of lifestyle modification. He furthered his briefing with a discussion of the role of the central nervous system. It was explained that the CNS consisted of the brain and spinal cord with the role of controlling every action in our entire body. From the beating of the heart, to the spasm of a muscle, tiny little spinal nerves exiting from the windows between every vertebrae or spinal bone were destined to control a specific part of our body.

Dr. Smith mentioned something called optimal health. That to achieve optimal health it would mean that the body would have to have 100% of its communicating capacity through the CNS and nothing less! Due to the profound function of the CNS, optimal health was extremely important in our lives because daily stresses could create an unbalanced CNS. Things like physical trauma, repetitive movements, poor posture, mental/emotional stress and toxins from the food, water and air we put into our bodies. All had the ability to alter our nervous system function and hence our bodily expressions. The results could pay heavy on our health in the long run. And for most of us it already had.

Dr. Smith spoke about the body as a whole. Servicing it with proper exercise, adequate nutrients, stress relief, regular spinal checks, positive mental outlook, clean water, dental care and yearly physical exams. The formula he called a lifestyle. To achieve our own individual optimal potential Dr. Smith and his wellness staff would be monitoring our nervous systems and musculoskeletal systems. We would be working closely with Dr. Smith, massage therapists, acupuncturists, reflexologist's and naturopathic doctors to achieve a balance in our bodies. Dr. Smith emphasized that it was the programs goal to lead its graduates not only in fending off an addiction to dangerous chemicals but to find a drug-free way of life that meant no looking back.

As the introductions continued we finally had the opportunity to head to the cafeteria for breakfast. However, the last thing on my mind was food. Indeed, I was frail, tired and malnourished. But starving I was not although the food looked very inviting. Before we were allowed to frequent the buffet we would have to listen to the center's nutritional expert. She was thorough in her discussion of the centers dietary guidelines used to help our nutrient deprived bodies. Furthermore, she mentioned that those battling substance abuse lack the essential vitamins and nutrients necessary to maintain optimal health. It was clear that we would benefit from organic meats, fruits and vegetables. We would also be avoiding synthetic foods, inflammatory agents, excess sugars and toxic preservatives. She concluded by reminding us of our individual dietary consultations that would be taking place later that day. They would be conducted to ensure that we were getting everything we would need on the road back to health and for the future to come.

I had visions of a psychiatric hospital where its patients were repetitively drugged with medications to mask their problems. However, the centers focus was quite the opposite. In fact, the goal was to show us how to combat our addictions thereby being armed with the knowledge to lead a completely healthy, drug free life. And it also included the use of pharmaceutical-based medications unless otherwise necessary.

My appetite was as weak as my body. However, my urgency to eat just wasn't there. The medical doctor I had met with the previous night stated that a side-effect of the medication I was on was a loss of appetite. And hungry I was not. The food on the other hand looked spectacular. I could hardly wait until I felt ready to eat. The choices were plentiful but nothing caught my eye on that day. I made a small attempt at forcing down some fruit but my digestive tract resisted all the way. Everything from taste, texture and smell put me off. I could only hope it was the withdrawal medication that funneled this unlikely occurrence because I loved to eat. I managed to wrestle with some toast before choking down some juice as a visitor sat down next to me. It was Tom once again.

"So what do you think so far, Michael?" He asked.

To be honest it is all a bit overwhelming.

"Substance abuse is definitely that way with your life. So is fighting back from the initial shock that your body will be experiencing. It won't be long until you start to see the bigger picture."

So what is on the agenda for the rest of the day, I asked.

"Every morning begins at 5:30 a.m. in the gym. Up to 8 a.m. you will be working with Dr. Smith and his team of wellness experts. Then you get an hour to clean up following breakfast until group addiction counseling begins. Following lunch you will spend some time with our psychologist, psychiatrist and the individual addiction counselor after that. Next is a one-hour reflection time before dinner. After dinner tonight you have a very special speaker. Every night something motivating takes place to reward you for all of your efforts. And that is the protocol around here barring a few exceptions, Michael."

So what are the exceptions? I asked.

"Well, for starters every Tuesday and Thursday in May you will be working with a life coach for several hours during the day and Sunday's you get to sleep in until 8 a.m."

Great, I replied is a less than enthusiastic tone. I took a quick glance at my watch. I suppose I better get ready for my meetings this afternoon, Tom.

"I will definitely see you tonight Michael. Enjoy the day!"

So off I went on a trek to my room to prepare for the remainder of my day. After leaving the company of Tom my curiosity started to grow regarding the infamous clinic director. I couldn't help but wonder what his role entailed? It surely wasn't common practice for surf-bums to seek employment at a world-class rehabilitation center, I thought.

Later that afternoon, at the group addiction session I prepared myself for the preaching that I believed would ensue regarding the dangers of drug addiction. However, much to my amazement I met an array of young people from all over the globe just like me. Somewhere along the way they too chose the wrong path in life. Each individual indeed had a story to tell in relation to his or her capture in despair! A load to get off of their chest even in front of strangers they had never met. After all it appeared to be a safe place to narrate the events that unfolded.

I was literally blown away by some of the dialogue. Taken aback by the subject matter. There were many people who shared a similar story to mine surrounding me. It was the first time in my life that I was able to view my own ego-dominated, sense of self in the works. I never thought that anyone else could possibly be living in the same confines as I was. Yet again, my ego blocked the true view of the world around me. I was truly feeling awestruck by the whole experience that afternoon.

I was astounded by the first-hand accounts that I was subjected to. Individuals who were victims of physical abuse from their loved ones. Other's who were sexually abused and even threatened by their parents. There were stories of suicide, murder and criminal activity. In actuality, it became more so apparent that my story didn't hold a candle to the many others I heard. It was during this experience that I continually felt myself shrinking smaller and smaller with every version that I listened to. Each story chiseled at the cemented chip sitting atop my shoulder. Dr. Marshall was dead right in saying that my sense of self clouded my cognition from the world around me. I was beginning to see the truth, as I was touched, even to the point of tears, on many occasions that day.

I think that one story hit me the hardest. A wealthy teenage girl bore her soul to the listeners in the group. She explained being born into a filthy rich family with a mother that was addicted to drugs. Throughout the course of her pregnancy her mother was using heavy doses of heroine which subjected the teenager to birth complications. Firstly, the girl was lucky to have been born at all as the mother's drug use was toxically damaging the babies development. Barring the effects of heroin on pregnancy the girl was born 2 months early through a c-section. It was the only procedure used to offer the girl a fighting chance. However, the medical staff at the time was skeptical the girl would even make it past the delivery. She was brutally underdeveloped physically. Severely depleted of the proper nutrients necessary to develop her susceptible immune system. In essence, she was a target for countless bacteria to attack her immune deficient infantile frame. And they bombarded her from day one. The girl not only battled the premature status thrust upon her at birth but she fought off rheumatic heart disease, pneumonia and severe liver complications.

Essentially, the teenage girl was born into the world to fight for her life. However, the fight would continue long after her birth. Not only born addicted to heroine the girl had a mother who thought of her as an illegitimate child. The girl grew up underdeveloped due to her mother's negligence and was unaccepted by her family. Raised by the household staff hired to care for her the girl became subjected to her mothers abuse, neglect and addictions. The entire journey led her to suicide attempts, severe depression and drug abuse. Now at eighteen years of age the teenage addict who had battled her entire life found enough inner strength to know that the process didn't have to continue. She wanted to find inner peace by ending the suffering she herself was implementing on her life. Never once blaming her predicament for her demise she had come to the center to accomplish the goal of becoming clean in order to live life based on her terms. Her provocative account smashed through the tough exterior surrounding my heart. In fact, it made me angry.

However, the experience I witnessed forced a number of emotions upon me that made me forget about myself for hours. It showed me that other people existed in this world other than just myself. People that share in the same experience and suffering that I did. I didn't think it was at all possible because I thought of myself as the only thing that mattered on the planet. It wasn't hard to understand that my ego had misled me.

After lunch my demeanor had totally shifted regarding the entire experience. I felt like a lost man who finally woke up from an endless nightmare. Following lunch I was ready for the task of having my head invaded by the staff psychiatrist. Then it would be my past that was analyzed by the staff psychologist. Despite my resistance the meetings went surprisingly well. The headshrinkers were very friendly and polite in asking me what seemed like a thousand different questions. I had tried to answer most of the questions with shortened responses as I was starting to feel the fatigue of the eventful day. I was emotionally drained from the group meeting that was held earlier. So by the time I had reached the psychologist her analytical business like approach made it difficult to establish a connection at that time. So naturally she backed me into a corner that prevented me from opening up to her.

The one-on-one addiction counseling was next to come that afternoon. Feeling the effects of the brain-drain from the first day of the program I wasn't looking forward to any more meetings. However, my "know it all attitude" came back to the forefront. Going into the meeting the chip was back on my shoulder. I was armed and dangerous yet again. But the young lady I was partnered with turned my attitude around. She was a great mediator. No preaching. No heavy statistical numbers. No threats. It was a peaceful conversation that revolved around life in general. It was real. In fact, it was just like the entire day had been.

The center was full of real people with a genuine concern for my overall well being. Something that I definitely hadn't been accustomed too! After all I came from a world where people told you exactly what you wanted to hear. It wasn't real in any sense of the word. So unlike my regular life the experience at the center broke that focus by presenting the opposite end of the spectrum. Opening my eyes to an entirely different world that other people inhabited. In doing so the activities that I engaged in kept me from considering the option of snorting cocaine and drowning in alcohol. As astounded as I was I believe my mind was opening up to the other possibilities that existed for a life of actual meaning.

Later that day I used the quiet time I was granted to lay out on the manicured lawn of the courtyard basking in the warm sunlight. It was peaceful, cozy and sheltered from the ocean breeze. Most of all, it enabled me to reboot my depleted battery. It was evident that mentally and physically the day's schedule had led me to exhaustion. The peaceful time alone was something that I was typically unfamiliar with during the normal course of a business day and it surprisingly felt great. However, I was interrupted from my moments of peace by a soft voice greeting me.

"Good afternoon, Michael. Soaking up some of those fine California rays I see."

It was Tom the mysterious clinic director. He looked a little different from his normal appearance as he held a briefcase in his hand. It would have been more appropriate to see him holding a surfboard.

So tell me your story, Tom, I asked.

"My story?" Tom replied.

Yes! Everyone I have met here today has a story.

"I suppose they do and I am certainly no different Michael."

So when do I get to hear about the crazy clinic director at the ocean side rehabilitation center?

"I would love to stay and chat but my duty calls at the moment, Michael. I have a meeting to attend in the next five minutes. So we will address my story in the near future. Sorry about that."

I understand. So maybe another time, I laughed.

"I want to remind you not to miss tonight's talk," he shouted as he left the courtyard. "It is going to be very powerful!"

And off he went to carry out his business. I was left again to continue pondering my life decisions in the radiance of the afternoon sun. I replayed the images of my wife and daughter playing alone in the waves at the beach. The pictures I saw furthered to the milestones of my daughter, Eva. Seeing her learning to walk, beginning to ride a bike and even graduating from school had all entered my mind. These were all milestones that I was never around to see. The field expanded even further as I saw Eva learning to drive a car, going to the high school prom and going off to college. Not one of the images that overtook my mind showed me anywhere in site.

I had chosen to remove myself from these important life moments. I hadn't thought of their meaning until now. So I began to cry as the pictures continued to revolve over and over again in my head. It was a release I suppose. However, the images were beautiful to witness. In fact, many of these events had already taken place without my bearing witness. And it hurt. Finally, something I was able to see other than my own relentless pursuit for power. It was a breath of fresh air to change the order of my thoughts. Something that hadn't happened for quite some time! And as much as it hurt it was a good thing for me to recognize.

At 7:30 p.m. that evening I labored my exhausted body to the theatre to take in the special presentation that had been promoted by Tom. The theater was filled with the numerous guests that I had spent most of my day with and many others that I didn't even recognize. Most of the staff was present also. And much to my surprise Dr. Marshall returned to take in the proceedings as well. As I looked around the room I could see Dr. Marshall and Tom conversing behind a podium set up for the speaker. My mind toggled with the questions I had regarding Tom's character in all of this. However, my thoughts passed soon after as I directed my attention to the guest speaker to come.

As the room went silent Tom approached the podium. He attached a mobile microphone to his suit jacket and wandered into the crowd of onlookers. The first thing that caught my eye was that Tom had traded in his usual shorts, Hawaiian shirts and flip-flops for a flashy suit and tie. Immediately, Tom the surfer dude by day turned into a businessman by night. He opened the ceremony referring to an experience he encountered with a young man in the courtyard that afternoon. He detailed the young man wanting to know his personal story and how horrible he felt by leaving that person that afternoon without sharing a powerful piece of himself.

Tom continued by mentioning that everyone has a story. All of us, including him! In fact, he mentioned that all stories had been written with the premise of being told! So tonight was his opportunity to tell his tale. It turned out that the guest speaker that night was Tom, the clinic director. He was going to open his heart and his life by sharing his story with us. A group of total strangers.

Tom began by making reference to a young man that he knew who had been born into a family of great privilege. A family that had high expectations of its members. He told of a young man that had it all at his fingertips. The money, material and power were endless. Since he was old enough to drive the young man drove disgustingly expensive luxury automobiles. He had access to winter and summer vacation homes around the world. The finest of clothes and the best in education were all provided. However, he acknowledged his appreciation for all that he was born into. Unlike, many of his counterparts born of great wealth the young man exemplified gratitude to his family.

Like most of what the young man had to offer nothing seemed to satisfy his parents. Nothing was good enough to please them. In fact, it became so bad that his parents started to dictate the important life choices that would ultimately direct his life. Things like college. Even the subject of study! And the career path he needed to take. All of which the young man agreed to do in order to make his family proud! A great sacrifice you might say.

Eventually, the young man graduated from Princeton atop his class with a degree in science. After receiving his degree it was his dream to travel the globe before settling down into a career. So he announced his plans to his parents. Unfortunately, the dictatorship forced upon the young man once again derailed his plans of adventure. Instead, he was pressured into applying to medical schools across the country or else he would be cut off from the trust fund his parents held so high above his head. It was medicine that they thought would be the image that best suited their son. It was what they wanted. Once again, to meet their wishes the young man enrolled in medical school. Giving up on what he wanted out of life.

Without an inkling of desire he continued his academic success far away from the ruling powers that controlled his every move. However, the pressure from his parents continued mounting, as did the added weight of a heavy curriculum. It had all been building for years. The stress and strain placed on the young man's heavy heart in regards to his parents meddling. And when it finally reached the breaking point the mistakes began to follow. In order to blow off the pressures of medical school the young man found refuge in partying with friends. At first it was the typical college nights of drinking and having fun. Next, it became serious. The occasional party nights started to become regular and then consistent. It wasn't long before occasional drinking became binging. However, one slip led to another as more emphasis was placed on the excess partying than on attaining an education. So less time studying translated into a lower grade point average. It wasn't long before the pressures from home reached an all time high as his grades were ultimately revealed.

To manage the best of both worlds the young man was introduced to the use of pharmaceutical amphetamines. That way he could party all night and study all day. Fulfilling what he believed was his desire for fun and his parent's wishes for him to become a physician. It wasn't long until the demands on his life became difficult to manage. The frequency of the drinking escalated from weekends to weeknights. Sometimes even the nights before major examinations! It was evident that drugs and alcohol took precedents over school. Maybe because they were the escape from reality that he felt he needed. Perhaps a safe haven to get out from under his parents continuous control!

Fortunately, along the way the young man met a beautiful girl enrolled in the same program. There friendship grew from casual drinking buddies into a bonafide love affair. She too came with a troubled past so together they immersed themselves in the destructive toils of addiction. All along the way the two managed to hide their addictive ways from family, classmates, friends and teachers. However, they were indeed similar in every human sense. They were obviously empty on the inside. Depleted of the driving forces that life had to offer.

Ironically the young man had become somewhat interested in the field of psychiatry. In fact, he set out to seek a psychiatric residency in his hometown bringing the love affair to a crossroads. The two had some serious decisions to make regarding the direction of their lives. He had to make his parents happy! But he wanted to keep the only friend he had in his life also. In the end the young girl accepted a residency at a local children's hospital nearby his hometown. That way the two could continue the relationship they had started. The young mans parents purchased a house for him on his arrival home. However, what they didn't know was that the girl he had been dating had also moved in. Much to their disapproval the two went about their ways of working and partying until the early hours of the morning.

For blundering his parents plan the young man was disowned. His mother and father mounted an attack to inadvertently steer the young man in the directional course that they believed appropriate. A young woman of modest means would not unite with the wealth and power of their own. So in spite of their wishes to contain the family blood lines the young man ignored their dominance. For his resistance he was thrown out of their lives. They refused to acknowledge him from that point on. His trust fund was legally revoked. His parents literally wiped his face with the decision during the legal proceedings. However, without a bank account of comparable means the young mans refute went softly by the wayside.

For all of his troubles in attempting to live a life with the premise of making his parents happy he had been left with nothing. The young man abandoned his own dreams. His own passions! His own life in the process! In fact, his sacrifices only served to entrench him deeper in a life that he didn't want to live. For this he harbored a definitive anger for giving up his own dreams. Emotionally distraught, encountering a constant internal conflicting dialogue the young man turned to the only escape he knew of at the time. Drugs and alcohol were the tools he used to leave the pain he perceived. In the process he extended an invitation to some local friends to join him in what he coined his "going away party." Even though he wasn't physically planning on going anywhere. With the party around him the young man had a mission that night. The alcohol was in excess. The drugs were even more dangerous than the usual menu he ordered from. And the mindset was one of mental torture. Together the young man and his girlfriend numbed their pain before being led to the nightlife of the local scene.

At a dance club they continued the fall from reality that they began so many hours before. The young man understood the purpose of the journey but the girl perhaps did not. At about 4 a.m. the young man was removed from the premises for being too intoxicated to speak or stand. Instead, he and his love were escorted home by the establishment's courtesy limousine. Upon arriving home it was just like any other return from a night of indulgence. Together they passed out in bed.

Hours had flown by before any rustle of the impaired body's had taken place. The young man finally awoke late that afternoon due to the sound of his hospital beeper going off. Amidst his nauseated state he realized that he had missed his shift at the local hospital and hurried to the phone to announce his whereabouts. Beside all the chaos the young girl remained quiet in peace. She was seemingly motionless for a long period of time as the young man carried about his business. All of which went unnoticed by him.

Too hung-over to attend to his unconscious girlfriend the young man allowed her to continue her slumber as he went downstairs in search of food. Hours later he returned to the side of his young love. In an attempt to wake her he was presented with the horrifying reality that she wasn't responding. In fact, not only had the girl been unconscious for hours but she wasn't breathing either. With no pulse or respiration the young man dialed 911 before attempting to revive the girl from what seemed like a coma. When the EMS team arrived at the house they examined the girl only to conclude that she was dead at the scene.

Later on at the hospital an autopsy and toxicity-screen revealed the cause of death. Much to the amazement of the young man it was concluded that the girl died due to an overdose of drugs and alcohol. The women he had loved, his best friend through school, in life and during their escapes had made her own

76

dramatic exit. The young man was obviously heart broken. Left blaming himself for her demise! An onslaught of feelings that would confront him for many years to come!

At that point in the compelling story that Tom had told I looked on with a blank stare. Simply, because the story could have easily been written for me. I not only endangered my life but I could have easily subjected someone to the same dangerous lifestyle I called my own. Tom was very emotional as he continued explaining the young man's long period of remorse that had turned to a deep, dark, depression. The young man was left with nothing. His parents abandoned him. The friends he had were false. He was a struggling student with no financial means to support him. Everything looked bleak at that time.

The story became even worse when the police initiated their investigation into the mysterious death of the young girl! Over the next several months the young man was stripped of his residency position at the hospital until further notice pending the investigation. He lost his credibility with the people of the town. There wasn't a place around where he could go that people weren't adding chapters to the drama regarding his scenario. The town residents who believed he was responsible for the death of his girlfriend openly threatened the young man! He eventually lost his home because he couldn't afford the payments and his car was repossessed. The young man was penniless. Homeless! Waiting in anticipation of the results from the police investigation. At the time he believed prison seemed like a viable solution. At least he would have shelter over his head and regular meals throughout the course of a day. Something he struggled for during that time! No one cared to be associated with him after the events unfolded. He was alone in the darkness that had become his life.

As Tom continued he described that the investigation conducted by the local authorities cleared the young man from any criminal acts regarding the death of his girlfriend. However, in searching the young man's residence the police found evidence of illicit drugs and paraphernalia relating to their addictive ways. In fact, the police were readying to pursue trafficking charges before the arrival of the young mans grandfather. It was the only family member that the boy had remained in contact with over the years despite the fact that is grandfather lived in Europe.

Hearing about his grandson's recent turmoil he returned home to be by his side. With his influential contacts the grandfather was able to halt the unnecessary investigation around his grandson's case. Instead, all criminal charges were dropped with the entrance of the young man into a rehabilitation facility. Furthermore, the young man was offered the return of his residency upon successful completion of the program.

It was a turn of events that reconnected him to his family. Finally, he had a friend in his life. Someone who could help redirect his current course. Clean and sober upon completion of his rehabilitation the young man was instilled with a new passion that he had never quite witnessed before. While in the treatment facility he observed the clinical application of human development in regards to addiction by a young resident named Dr. Marshall. It was this energy that led to his graduation as a medical doctor specializing in psychiatry.

Following years of clinical psychiatry the young man grew tired of depressing hospitals, over medicated patients, crashing health care systems and tiresome schedules. Instead, he revisited his application of using his interest of psychiatry in the field of addiction management. However, he furthered this interest to designing an addiction program centering on not only physical health and mental but also personal development. He believed that a distinct connection existed between the mental and physical persona of a person battling an addiction because of numerous imbalances that had unraveled within their lives.

The young man spent several years developing a conceptual model that would revolutionize the world of drug rehabilitation. After seeking countless attempts at institutionalizing his program the young man seemed to falter. However, there was one last investor that wanted to hear his pitch. In fact, the same potential investor had been conducting decades of business dealings around the world and was always ready to diversify his money. The presentation was a success. The young man not only secured the financial backing necessary to make his vision become real he had also been provided with a substantial property with which to construct the image he created. His grandfather once again believed his grandson was destined for something far greater than wandering the halls of a medical facility. He too saw the vision and invested in it. With the full support of his grandfather the substance abuse center in his mind became an absolute reality.

It became a place to help people repair their broken lives and renew the love for life that had been lost through a holistic approach to health. A venue for those encountering drug and alcohol addictions whose lives require mending in the other facets of life beyond that of just chemicals! A program beyond the focus of the vehicles used to escape the actual causes of the problems that appear to be real.

Once again emotionally charged Tom stated "That is my story."

"My dream has come to fruition through the fortunate turn of events that offered me a second chance at life. It was my life but I couldn't see it until I learned about the similar encounters my grandfather had experienced while he was growing up. He enabled me to see that it was my life I was living, not a life for someone else. So I took it back. I learned some deadly lessons along the way. I traversed the depths of darkness beyond what most feel incomparable to their lives. I turned a nightmare into a dream making that very same dream come true with the help of my beloved grandfather."

"Tonight, you are all standing with me in that dream. I saw the vision in my dreams for years. I just had to see through the shadows that were blocking my way. I will be forever grateful to my grandfather for seeing in me something that took years for myself to see. However, that has all changed. I understand whom I really am even now that my grandfather has left the world. We still converse every night when I rest my head on my pillow. He is with me in these halls and everywhere at all times. It is a story that could easily be yours. My story. A painful but purposeful journey on the road called life that I continue each and every day I am here on earth. A journey that I relive each and every night I share my story with the people that visit the center I have created. However, albeit an important thing to honor your past because of the valuable lessons that help pave the future of our lives, it is also necessary for you to acknowledge the present."

"You have all obviously realized that you want more for your lives or else you wouldn't be here in my presence. You have chosen to take the first step, as did I, to get your lives back on the direction that you believe they should be. And you will! You must come to knowing where you are in your life at present. You were meant to travel these roads for a reason that will become all together clear during your stay here at the center. For without acknowledging your present you cannot change what the future holds for you."

"My program is about so much more than drug and alcohol addiction. We cannot place the blame on a single chemical creation alone because we as people make decisions to incorporate them in our lives. Why? To escape the various things that we choose to ignore that surround us. Whether it's the pressures of money, the stress of relationships, a failing marriage, a hurtful past, a fearful future or a doubtful existence we use various means to escape. A life that may not have been going the way you'd hoped. The life you can and will have if you just confront it. A life you always dreamed about with the people, places and things you have always been able to envision. The life you were born to live when your parents brought you into the world. I stand here telling my story to you as a prime example of the many that have won a major victory in life."

"I turned a perceived tragedy into triumph and you all can do it too. I assure you that it is a very real possibility because I am no different than you. It will happen. It can happen. You just have to open your heart to the process as it unfolds. When the student is ready, the teacher will appear."

"My role at the center is to be your life coach. Inside you are all the answers you will ever need to get your life back on the road you would like to travel. I will help you find those answers within yourself. I am honored to be a part of your life and especially look forward to being a part of each and everyone of your growth in the time you will spend in reaching your ultimate potential. The early goings can be tough. It's not easy removing the barriers to your personal growth. But as you know from listening to my story tonight you can see the tides can turn. And I am confident because of my work with hundreds of people before you that you will witness the same. Thank you for listening to my life story and understanding that I am no different from you. Life is your journey. It goes where you want it to go. I am just the guide that helps you find what lies within you during a very special 'Eight Days In May'."

At the completion of his heartfelt talk I suddenly had all of the answers I had been searching for regarding the man behind the center. It was real. It was all very real. That is the feeling I had as I left the auditorium that night. A sensory overload that I had been completely unfamiliar with for quite some time. Suddenly, I was able to see the opportunity I had been introduced to. I finally had clarity in relation to the journey I was suppose to take and the guide that would accompany me. The journey and the guide were revealed right in front of my very own eyes!

Reflection

"The average man who does not know what to do with his life,
wants another one which will last forever."
-Anatole France-

I will never forget the events leading to the realization that my lifestyle could wind up in dangerous territory. During a meeting in early April, not long after I separated from my wife and daughter I was summoned to the office of Robert Stanwick.

As the CEO of I-Global Robert was eager to discuss with me the latest trends taking place in the technology industry in Asia. Robert was a visionary much like myself, so we could talk for hours on end about business. Robert was set to leave that evening for Hong Kong once the company jet was given the okay to fly. In a non-formal meeting prior to his departure we guzzled a half dozen glasses of scotch before I enlightened Robert on the current market in Asia.

Throughout most of our meetings we were usually taken care of by Robert's executive secretary, Jennifer. There was no arguing that she ran the show. The young, bold, beautiful 28-year old had the energy and poise necessary to keep Robert on schedule. At that moment we were lighting cigars when Jennifer returned from Robert's office for a brief conversation. As they conversed I admired the lush confines of Robert's suite. The walls were lined with cherry wood. He sat behind an Italian designed eighteenth century desk. For relaxation he had a sofa and chairs made from the finest leather facing a large plasma television mounted over his credenza on the wall. As they talked I took in the brilliance of what it meant to become a corporate giant. In fact, the reality was that I could see myself sitting in Robert's office one day soon.

It turned out that Robert had to get up to the roof to catch a helicopter to the airport. I understood from their conversation that Robert's flight time to Hong Kong had been bumped forward and he had to catch the chopper in order to be on time. As Jennifer prepared Robert for his exit I remained seated with a full glass of scotch and a half smoked Cuban cigar. At that very moment Jennifer returned with a full glass of wine and wondered if I would have any trouble with her joining me.

The two of us shared in several cocktails as we chatted for hours about the numerous odds and ends of life when Jennifer mentioned she would be meeting some friends at a local pub later that evening. Naturally, she extended an invitation for me to accompany her and I accepted. I had absolutely nothing else on my agenda that evening and drinking with a friend was certainly more appealing than drinking alone.

The pub environment was packed with the after work crowd of San Francisco's business district. It was difficult to move and if you did you were sure to lose your spot, wherever that may have been. When we arrived Jennifer introduced me to her gang of friends. A mix of both men and women whose names I didn't care to memorize. In fact, I really didn't feel much like socializing in a loud bar with strangers. However, my mood was destined to change once a band began to prepare for their performance.

When the band had hit the stage I grabbed Jennifer and off we went to the dance floor. Certainly at that point I had consumed enough alcohol to calm my nerves so dancing was definitely an option. It wasn't long until many offers piled up on my dance card. However, in order to continue the necessary energy I would need some performance enhancement. So off to the restroom I disappeared. Being relaxed was a great state but I needed the endurance that cocaine could provide me. Only then would I continue to be a dancing machine!

As the evening progressed I was having a blast. Of course, anytime I was drunk and stoned I was having fun. However, most of it became a blur. There was a ton of drinking and countless trips to the restroom for little "pick me ups". I met the many single ladies that were on hand and danced with a few unknowns along the way. These were the only details I could recall from the events of that night.

My watch alarm as usual woke me up the morning after at 5 a.m. Like usual I was met with a pounding headache, a dry mouth and blurry vision. In a half conscious state I rolled over in what I thought was my bed to hear the mumble of a woman sleeping beside me. And that is when it hit me. Where was I? Who was sleeping beside me? Frantically, I hit the nearest light switch in anticipation that I was home with Lisa sleeping by my side. Much to my dismay I found that I was neither at home nor was it Lisa I was sleeping with. I was in what appeared to be a hotel room with a young woman I had never soberly seen before. It definitely wasn't my wife and all I could think about was Lisa.

As I tore out of bed I was in a panic. At least I was dressed in the same suit that I had on the day before. I knew there was a change at the office. But the fact that I was clothed meant that it was less likely that I offended my marriage to Lisa. Groggy from the late night exploits I quietly looked back at the bed shaking my head in disbelief. It was an all time low even for me. To not know where you are is a pretty dangerous turn of events. So I didn't want to wait around long enough to find out who the young woman was or what we hand done.

On my way to the hotel elevator I thought about the scene I had just escaped from. It wasn't even the obvious questions that entered my mind. Questions like, who was I sleeping beside? Instead, it was one profound question. Was my excessive behavior becoming too much for even my control? I knew for sure that on that particular night something had changed. Never had I woken up in a strange place with an unrecognizable person beside me.

It was certainly an internal conversation that I would be having with myself for some time to come. However, the answers were destined to arrive much later! Nonetheless, it was the first of many moments in my already destructive life that raised a serious red flag. It wasn't the all night drinking, the consumption of an illegal drug or the notions of sexual behavior that provoked it. However, waking up with absolutely no recognition of the previous nights events with a stranger in a mysterious place was rendering my actions uncontrollable. So that is where I consciously observed for the first time my descent into the unknown world I sought refuge in. Even long before my admission that I was in trouble.

Chapter Six:
The First Day in May:
Acknowledging What You Are

"Hidden away in the inner nature of the real man is the law of his life, and someday he will discover it and consciously make use of it. He will heal himself, make himself happy and prosperous, and live in an entirely different world. For he will have discovered that life is from within and not from without."
-Ralph Waldo Emerson-

It was Tuesday May the first. The day after I learned the shocking revelation behind the story of Tom. Much like my entire first day in the program I was blown away by the dramatic account of his past. Tom's story was incredibly riveting. One that we could all relate with to some extent. After all each individual in the program had already battled against the odds to shift the course of their lives in the direction of the center. It was comforting to know that the man behind the entire program understood what it meant to walk in the same shoes as his current participants. As opposed to preaching to us from the contents of a "How to Sober Up" manual! It wasn't hard to see that Tom really cared and above all else wanted to establish a connection with each person enrolled in his program.

What continued to intrigue me even was Tom's role as a life coach. I wasn't even sure what a life coach really meant when I first heard the designation. However, what I did know at that point was that every Tuesday and Thursday in May I would be meeting with Tom to find out more. It was strange. I was actually looking forward to the next step on my journey at the center, but I really didn't know why? Maybe the "Eight Days In May" I would be spending with my life coach would provide me with the necessary answers I was seeking. And that is how I would leave it for the time being.

As the afternoon rolled around I was making my way to the reception desk to inquire the whereabouts of Tom's office when I came upon Louisa.

Hello Louisa! I said.

"Mr. Jamieson how can I help you," she replied.

I was wondering how I could find Tom's office as I have a meeting with him this afternoon.

"Yes, that is a very popular question," Louisa responded.

In that instant, Louisa surfaced from behind the desk she seemed all too familiar with and guided me towards the front entrance of the center lobby. From the entranceway she pointed towards a large stretch of beach overlooking the Pacific Ocean.

"Tom's office is located down there on the beach," She said.

Down on the beach? I replied in disbelief.

"On the beach Mr. Jamieson," she insisted.

I was very confused. What kind of office is that?

"Just head on down and you'll be sure to find Tom waiting for you, Mr. Jaimeson."

Interesting, I thought in regards to having an office located on the beach. What kind of meeting was this going to be? So, anxious to move on with the afternoon proceedings I traversed my way down the protective cliffs characteristic of the Monterey area to meet Tom in his sanctuary on the beach. It was a warm, windy afternoon and the beach was empty. Not a soul in sight, except of course for Tom.

Appropriately adorning the beach attire I was accustomed to seeing him wear, Tom greeted me with a friendly smile and welcomed me to his office away from the office.

"Michael, welcome to my office," he proclaimed.

It is obviously a metaphor I assume!

"Isn't it beautiful down here?"

Oh, without question it has a great view.

"It is a unique comparison to the places we normally associate with conducting our business isn't it?"

I suppose it is very different from the normal work environment we associate with.

"Yes! No phones, computers, people or chaos. No distractions. A fabulous place to retreat to get things accomplished."

What kind of things? I asked him.

"Patience, Michael," Tom replied.

"Today is the first day in May and as your life coach we have a great many topics to discuss."

What is a life coach anyway? I asked eager to find some answers.

"Good question, Tom replied. A life coach is someone who becomes a mentor of sorts in a person's life journey. A friend that understands where you've been and were you want to go. And also how to get there! Usually, your coach is a person that has made many of the same mistakes along the way that you have. One who is capable of helping you avoid those same pitfalls to prevent unnecessary disaster along the way. A person that can offer insight in your search for the answers to your life! The answers that reside within you."

Thank you! That makes complete sense to me, Tom.

"I hope you understand my role in all of this, Michael. I have certainly been in your shoes and I have considered letting go of everything just as you have. However, the reality is that there are so many perfect things in the world worth seeing and experiencing. It would be a shame for you to miss out on the gift that has been granted to you."

The world we live in is hardly perfect, I spouted back.

"I sense a little anger behind that statement, Michael."

It has been a tough road thus far I will admit.

"Ah, but the universe is 100% perfect. You just can't see it at the moment but you will in time."

I see poverty struck countries, plagues of disease, death from wars and political disaster!

"I understand your views of the world."

That is what I see when I pick up a newspaper or watch the news. I see anything but perfection.

"You see what you want to see, Michael," Tom stated.

What does that mean?

"When you look in the mirror, Michael, what do you see?"

I see myself, I remarked sarcastically.

"That's all you see when you stare into the mirror?" Tom stated with a smile.

I believe I am looking at the lowliest form of a human being that could possibly inhabit the earth if you really want to know, I stated in a serious tone to his question.

"Aha! You see exactly what your mind tells you to see," Tom shouted through the howling wind.

What are you talking about?

Tom pointed directly at me. "You see! What you see and what I see are two different things. I don't see the same Michael Jamieson that you do when you look into the mirror. Not at all! That is not who you truly are for a second!"

Well, than what should I see?

"Think for a minute, Michael. Look beyond your body! The flesh that houses your organs! Beyond the depths of your bones! What do you see?"

Nothing! I said in disappointment.

"Look deeper and you will find the answer to my question, Michael."

I don't know about that! It's pretty empty inside my body.

"Take a second and actually look deeper. Beyond the physical stuff you typically see. Beyond the big house, the fancy cars and important job title."

I guess I have a soul. The one I sold to the devil a long time ago, I said.

"Right! Now you are on the right track my friend. You see the entire planet we live on is made up of the same energy that comprises you. Your soul!"

Wait a minute! What energy? I yelled in confusion.

"An energy that is called universal intelligence. It resides in all living things including you," Tom replied.

With a sarcastic grin on my face I looked at Tom. Right! Whatever you say!

"Universal intelligence is the energy of the world that maintains the balance between order and chaos. If it wasn't around us to maintain order than things would be destructively flying around in chaos."

What are you talking about?

"A form of universal intelligence also lies within you. Its called innate intelligence and it is the energy behind "who" you are. Essentially, it is the soul that brings your earth suit to life!"

My earth suit? I questioned.

"Michael, you have to consider the energy that resides inside you. Some call it a spirit, others a soul and so forth. The innate energy connects the spiritual world, your soul, to the physical world, your body."

How so? I asked.

"It is the intelligence of your soul that holds the make-up of your character allowing the body it inhabits to come to life through expression. It's the you, that is in you!" Tom shouted.

So let me get it straight. I am a form of energy hiding behind a human body?

"Close Michael," Tom stated. "You are an infinite source of energy. The same energy that makes up the universe! You are limitless, eternal and housed within a human body until it is released through what the physical world calls death."

So when I die I return to the same form of energy that comprises the planet?

"Close Again! Without the intelligence your body is physically dead. The soul makes it come to life. By pumping the heart, taking oxygen to the lungs, digesting food, healing injuries, thinking and acting. The intelligence in you knows what to do."

How does it know all of this?

"Remember your encounter with Dr. Smith the other day?" Tom mentioned.

Yes, I replied. Why do ask?

"Recall for a second what you discussed, Michael."

You mean the interconnection of the brain and spinal cord that forms the CNS?

Now, Tom was smiling. "Yes the communicating network for your body and your life."

I am starting to see the point you are trying to make, Tom.

"Are you?"

Innate expresses itself through your CNS! It makes you laugh, digest your food, pumps the heart, heals a wound and allows you to love. It's the power that lets humans express themselves in this world.

"So when you flat lined the other day, lying in the hospital emergency room what would you say happened, Michael?" He asked.

I would say that my inner intelligence was restricted from expressing itself within the physical world! However, I still had some sense of consciousness in the realm I inhabited for that brief time. The problem was that I wasn't able to communicate in the manner I wanted to in the physical dimension that I sensed was vaguely within reach.

"So could we say that your innate intelligence, your soul, your spirit, whatever you want to call it, left your physical body during this time?"

I guess, I stated.

"Well, wait a second! Lets get it straight, Michael. Were you able to move your feet or your hands? Could you communicate with anyone? Were you hungry or tired?"

I see where you are going and the answer is no to all of your questions. When you break it down in that fashion I am certain that my soul had left my body while I was out cold.

"So if the innate left your body what happened to the corpse lying on the table during that time?"

I believe I was dead in the physical world, I said.

"You hit it right on the nose!"

What do you mean?

"You were dead in the physical sense of the word. Remember, the energy of your soul is infinite. It lives on forever in various forms. It is a part of all living things!"

So it carried on its business in the spiritual realm?

"Correct Again, Michael! The physical world is the world that we can see, hear, smell, taste and touch. But beyond these senses exists an entire world of energy that most people fail to acknowledge. And that is the spiritual world of energy!" Tom exclaimed.

Looking visibly confused I asked. Would that also be considered the after-life?

"You could call it something like that."

So I understand your points regarding what we are made of. The energy inside us is obviously amazing. But what I don't understand is how all of what we are discussing makes for a perfect world?

"Well, you see there is matter in all living things. If there weren't a universal energy in that matter maintaining order we would have things flying around uncontrollably in chaos. That is called Universal intelligence. It also functions inside you in the same capacity as innate intelligence."

So are bombs, disease and crime, all matter?

"No! Tom replied. The perfection exists in the balance that is in the world. It is in perfect order because the energy that maintains it is the same perfect energy that exists in all-living things! Its universal!"

So from what you are saying you would contend that we are all made up of the same energy?

"Now you are starting to see the bigger picture, Michael."

So we are all the same?

"In fact we are one!" Tom exclaimed. "The images of war, poverty, and disease are all circumstances of human perception, Michael. Just as you see an image of yourself, I see it differently."

So poverty to one person may be another person's wealth, I stated.

"Absolutely!"

So my miserable life predicament is someone else's success story?

"It's all what you make of it, Michael," Tom responded. "But the funny thing is that it's all in balance. For every bad thing you perceive in your life, something good also enters the picture to balance it. That alone defines the wonderful energy we are all made from."

And that is why you think it's perfect?

"No, Michael! That is what I know from my experience to be perfection. And you will find out for yourself very soon. However, we have to begin with a clean slate."

How so? I asked in intrigue.

"Seeing the perfection of the world, the perfection of your soul is a start. The elusive chase of money, titles, cars and wealth has nothing to do with actual perfection or success. It is certainly a relentless pursuit because the human mind believes we can never have enough stuff. However, it has nothing to do with the actual perfection that lies inside of us. The perfection you need to come to acknowledge."

A few moments of silence passed as Tom closed his eyes, sunning his face in the bright glowing sun. It was then that I had the sudden urge to summarize for myself something I had never truly contemplated. Life!

With what I have learned about the spiritual side of things how does God fit in to the entire picture?

"Your right, Michael! We've been discussing the spiritual realm. However, it is very different from the various religions that exist."

How so?

"People often intertwine the terms spiritual and religion. In fact, the two are totally separate entities. Make no mistake! A universal energy exists in all of us. The same energy that holds the world in a state of balance is in you doing the very same thing. Your innate, your spirit or your soul is maintaining the order within you as we speak. The energy we have been discussing has been called God, Allah, Buddha or Christ. Whatever you term it, it is still a universal energy synonymous with the energy governing the planet. It's infinite, boundless and limitless beyond the capabilities of the human senses. And that is what I call spiritual. It is your connection with the inner power that resides inside of you."

I see! I stated.

"Religion is something that has been manufactured through writings, teachings, traditions and history. Generations of civilizations have adhered to the rules of these religions as they have been passed down the ranks over the years. It's a practice based on the beliefs, commandments and guidelines that people acknowledge was created by one distinct, all mighty power of worship."

And that power is the energy called Universal Intelligence? I asked.

"You can call the universal power a god if you like but the source and its name is irrelevant. Much of the confusion between the terms spiritual and religion weigh in right here."

So religions have nothing to do with the spiritual?

"No, not at all! If people were only able to acknowledge that we are all made of the same infinite energy that balances the planet they would be able to put as much faith in themselves as they would the higher power they pray to."

Are you saying that god is within each and everyone one of us?

"You have already answered that question yourself, Michael."

As a spiritual being I guess a church or place of worship isn't necessary? I said sarcastically.

"All kidding aside, Michael, you do not have to go to church to be a spiritual person. You are already a spiritual being. Just recognizing that alone provides you with the distinction between that of organized religion."

So what of these colossal religious movements that created change amongst the world and its people?

"Hey, I am not for a moment going to extinguish the torch of change that has been lit by organized religion, Michael. No question religious movements have created major momentum through history. However, they have also been the cornerstone for war and violence."

So I can be a spiritual person in any old place, at any time?

"You can connect to your inner being anytime you like. And indeed you should! It is something that many people never have an opportunity to do," Tom stated.

That must be because they have no clue what it is we truly are, I replied.

We were surprisingly interrupted from continuing our conversation by a pod of dolphins that surfaced nearby our location. Tom and I rose to our feet the second they were spotted to observe the natural wonder first hand. They were wild and free with their effortless motions. Peaceful yet purposeful in their exploits in the ocean! We watched intently as they swam off into the distance to continue their journey. In the time of complete silence from words we were offered the sound of the wind and waves crashing against the coastline. And that is when Tom stood up waving his hands in the air as if to embrace what he could of the world around him.

In doing so, he looked at me and stated "You may not see it just yet, Michael, but that is an example of the perfection of the planet right in front of your very own eyes."

We paused for a moment to process the events.

"Michael, I can appreciate your eagerness to learn. Many people want as much information as they can get their hands on as soon as possible. In doing so they lose sight of the fact that life is a process."

A process?

"Yes, a process! And its one that I want you to enjoy each and every step of the way! In time you will learn to connect with your inner power. In fact, you will discover how you can express your true energy to the world you inhabit."

I just have to give it time I guess! Whatever it takes, Tom.

"Right now you are laying the foundation to be able to connect with your inner energy. Your soul! Your spirit! So to accomplish that we must first allow you the opportunity to digest what it is and what it does."

I understand the journey, I think!

"Come with me Michael," Tom stated.

We walked along the shoreline of Monterey beach taking in the gorgeous scenery that it offered. The beach itself was surrounded by an amphitheatre of fescue grass amongst mountains of century old water torn rocks. The seagulls soared above by the thousands in search of a mid-afternoon snack. The crash of the waves echoed through the strong but warm breeze as we carried on. While on our walk Tom explained how so many people in today's society are disconnected from their real selves.

He furthered his point by mentioning that society is so wrapped up in living out the expectations of others. The reason as he continued was the influence of sources close to them such as friends, family, teachers, religions and society. Tom concluded that people crave praise from those they feel are important influential figures in their lives. That society as a whole strives for acceptance through praise and recognition from others. That is what he coined meeting the expectations of others.

He explained that as children we are taught what to believe is possible or impossible. What is good or bad! So we set out from our breeding ground by acting and thinking similar to what we have been taught so we achieve the sense of acceptance through praise that we are striving for. Instead, we place ourselves at the mercy of others around us. What's worse is that we have placed our fate in the hands of our so-called peers and their hierarchy of expectations to be judged as they see fit. We all do it. We all seek love, acceptance, success and the warm fuzzy feeling we get from those who have judged us as doing the right thing.

However, as Tom continued he talked about how the dominating life course of chasing the expectations of others was merely a dark alley where human beings lose the connection to their true inner power. Failing to allow their real selves from being expressed to those around them. Instead, taking on the shape of a human presence that is anything but the true you. The focus of what I call a life "without" instead of being concerned about a life from "within."

Tom expanded the conversation to involve something he felt humans in general were put on this planet to do, the topic of a life from "within." And that involved expressing their inner spirits to the world. The true energy that occupied the rented human body! He discussed the expressions in human form were sub-grouped into numerous areas of the lives we tend to lead. Thus, he coined them the "Eight Cornerstones of Life". Tom described the "Eight Cornerstones" in great detail. They involved the areas of family, personal, financial, physical, mental/emotional, professional, social and spiritual. Tom referred to these as the cornerstones for human expression because we were designed to express our inner spirit to the physical world we occupy through these eight mediums. Furthermore, Tom mentioned that along the journey of life that many people become so emphatically lost in the cemented ideals of others that they sacrifice the most beautiful thing they have. And that is their connection between their spiritual and physical lives. Hence, the true expression of their real inner substance!

Tom held up two fingers. "Michael, there are two ways to express yourself in life."

Wait a second! I thought you mentioned eight areas that you called cornerstones?

"The cornerstones are mediums in your life where you have an opportunity to express your inner being to the physical life. What I am referring to is the vehicle you can choose to make that happen."

How so? I barked in eagerness.

"Through the use of your head or your heart," he replied.

At that point I was feeling a tiny bit overwhelmed with our discussion. I was trying to grasp as much information as possible but I needed clarification to make sure it was sinking in. Don't we use both the head and the heart in the physical life we live?

"Michael, we definitely use both. However, the large majority of people live from their heads."

So what is wrong with using your mind? From my experience most don't!

Tom broke into a brief giggle in response to my sarcastic remark regarding the fact that I felt most individuals on the planet fail to use their heads in getting on in their lives.

"Spending a large percentage of your time thinking, deciding, rationalizing, analyzing about your life course has a lot to do with the ideals set forth by generations before you."

So why do our minds do this?

"Simply, because it is a calculating process you have learned to use in order to make all of your life decisions to meet the expectations of others."

So I use all of my brainpower to make sure I am making the right decisions so that I will get the warm fuzzy feeling of being accepted rather than not by those around me?

"Yes, sir!" Tom stated.

And will spending all of that time in your head also wear you down? I questioned.

"Of course it does! But more importantly you become disconnected from your true self and its role in your physical journey. With a mind consumed with traveling down the path that others feel is the correct course to take you neglect the real power of the spirit inside of you."

So people never really get to see the true you?

"If your expressing yourself primarily using the vehicle of your head to the world in the eight cornerstones that concern your life there is absolutely no possibility that people are ever going to see the true you," Tom remarked.

So what do we see from these people than?

"Whatever they want you to see, Michael! It's a masquerade."

I am confused, I mentioned.

"If you are living mostly in your head it forces you to spend most of your time thinking about the past. Continuously questioning the future and what the ideals of our society believes are the manner in which you should conduct your life."

And that is what we do when we are in our heads?

"Your head is calculating the next step you will take. It knows you will be judged by those around you and even yourself for that matter on the choices you make along the way. So it initiates the cover up of who you really are and what you really want in your life because you are adhering to someone else's standards instead of your own."

That is what makes it impossible at times to let the real you come through! I said.

"It cannot go any other way if you are trying to be someone different in the eight cornerstones of your life, Michael."

From what you are saying it sounds as though we are dramatically acting through our lives.

"A very real statement, Michael," Tom replied.

It all makes sense when you take a step back for a moment.

"You know the theme of our visit today is to emphasize the balance that should exist in the world and in your life. It should include not only the energy but your expression of it," Tom remarked.

Well, if the balance is lost than chaos is able to rain free I suppose.

"Exactly, Michael. Just look around you! The entire human race has lost the concept of balance in adhering to the ideals set forth by others."

You mean it's not only the loss of balance between letting their real selves shine through and faking it to get by?

"Certainly not! Not only has the connection between the physical and the spiritual been overhauled by choosing a less efficient vehicle but the expression itself is in angst."

How so?

"In their attempts to chase down the path designed for them the actors in the fictional drama unfortunately forget how to balance the mediums they express themselves in."

So you are now referring to the eight cornerstones of life?

"Yes! Instead of placing equal value amongst the eight cornerstones individually the vehicle of their minds places priority on only a few and less of an importance on the rest."

Even I know that will create an imbalance in their lives.

"The real problem is that in the geographical location of the mind, the powerful ego also resides," Tom mentioned.

So is there some sort of clash as a result?

"When your ego or sense of self grows from your life experiences in the physical world it becomes a very powerful entity in your mind. It has the capacity to enlarge with your desire to chase after the standards of measure set by others. And it will judge you accordingly. Right or wrong! Good or bad! Your ego will reward and punish you every step of the way, if you let it."

The ego sounds like the catalyst in all of this, I remarked.

"The ego drives the vehicle of your mind as it yearns for the acceptance of ideals. It places value in material items, money, success and at the same time fogs your clarity for the other areas that must be kept in balance."

So the ego is what changes who you really are, if you let it?

"Only if you are disconnected, Michael! Many become disconnected because they get lost in their heads for far too long, succumbing to the power of their ego. Remember the balance? Tom Stated."

So neglecting the other areas within the important cornerstones will essentially cause turmoil in your life?

"Can you keep a balance in all eight cornerstones if you are prioritizing only a few? Can you create a balance if you only focus on one or two and neglect the rest?"

I do not see how that is possible!

"Well, you are right! It isn't possible if you are meant to express yourself from the important eight cornerstones that exist in your life and you neglect the majority of them in your quest to fulfill the expectations of others in spite of your own."

So the balance is lost! I stated.

"Michael, let me ask you something! Would you build a house that had a higher, stronger foundation at one end in relation to the other?"

Not a chance.

"Why?" Tom replied with a giant smile on his face.

Simply because the supporting structure would be deprived of any balance it required. It is an unbalanced home so to speak.

"So now you can understand your life is a house encasing the spiritual presence of the energy that comprises your being," Tom remarked.

If your not expressing that internal being equally amongst the eight cornerstones of life than its not hard to see how it can all fall apart.

"You are so right, Michael. However, remember it also depends on the vehicle you chose to drive the journey you're on," Tom replied.

Well, I can already see the relationship to my disastrous existence. I spend all of my time in my head allowing my ego to run wild. In fact, it has been driving my life in search of the stereotypical successful lifestyle I was seeking. You know the career, the material items and the money!

"Hey, people sacrifice a lot to strive to attain the ideals that others place importance in. Remember, you are taught that stuff from generations before you. That is what pads your ego to begin with. We've all experienced it! It's not hard to see how the perfection in the world gets so abruptly lost! People cannot understand the balance that exists because the ego speaks a different language."

So what about re-establishing the previously existing connection? I asked.

"The first step is to understand that you have lost the balance in your life. That is why you have ended up in a facility like this. The next step is to develop the internal knowing that you can live from a better venue instead."

I understand fully that my ego has clouded my better judgment in life. In fact, I let it destroy my life. I lost my family, my friends, my daughter, my health, my mind and nearly my life. After nearly losing everything that mattered I was left with an addiction to drugs, an affliction for chasing success and an ego that is out of control!

"There is no point in beating yourself up over the parts of a life that you have already lived," Tom replied.

Oh! Than what should I do? I asked in frustration.

Tom pointed straight at me. "Michael, take a look at what we've done here today for instance."

Well, for starters I guess you have opened my eyes to the tragedy I will call my life!

"Yes, but before today you never honestly saw your life consciously, did you?"

No, I can honestly say I did not!

"So what can you do with your new found vision to see the world?" Tom asked.

See it for what it is, I guess.

"Right, Michael! Put the past behind you knowing that a great lesson has been learned in those experiences. Then you will understand that there is more to the journey than the human eye can see."

Let me interrupt! I am the same energy that inhabits all living things on the planet.

"So stop thinking that you are different, for gods sake! In fact, you are no different than anyone else. No one on the planet is better than the person next to them. We are all the same so start treating people that way."

" If we are all made of the same energy than how can you look at someone differently?" The answer is you cannot! Because when you do, you are taking a shot at a piece of yourself."

You are so very right! I can see that our identities do not lie in our careers, our titles or our education, Tom.

"It's one world, Michael. A unity of energy from the same source."

I guess it would be a much better place if people realized that all that they needed to do was to crawl out from under the grasp of their ego!

"When you treat a banker different from the way you treat a street cleaner that is not you talking! When you tell business clients what you think they want to hear that is not you Michael, that is talking!"

Who is it then? I asked.

"It is you trying to portray the image of someone you are not."

And we do that because our ego tells us that is what we need to do to succeed?

"Remember, the ego in your head wants the validation, the credit and rewards instead of the pain that accompanies punishment."

That is why we become something we are not!

"Exactly, Michael!" Tom Said. "If all you do is where a mask all day with various people in different situations all you are really doing is faking your way through life."

I can admit that I am guilty of that, I said.

"Who isn't? And boy, let me tell you, it is a whole lot of work to portray an image of something you are not."

Is that why I am so tired all of the time?

"It is exhausting work, faking it!" Tom remarked.

"Michael, the truth is that you will never satisfy the expectations of the planet, its people or your loved ones because these are nothing but perceptions that have been handed down to them. They are fabrications of the human mind. By subjecting yourself to that kind of life you will find that your ego can never get enough. Whether you have a great career, lots of money in the bank, a big mansion with a Ferrari in the garage your ego can never have enough."

Sounds like a vacuum cleaner of sorts, Tom.

"People are always thinking about the next best thing!"

It sounds an awful lot like my life, Tom, I admitted.

"You just need to balance your life, Michael. There is no reason you cannot achieve and maintain a balance throughout the eight cornerstones that we express from. To do this you just have to let some of that real self of yours shine through the cracks. That, plus the fact that we also need to change vehicles!"

How do I do that?

"You don't have to avoid your head altogether, Michael," Tom said.

Just spend less time in it. I mentioned

"Your right! Just spend less time in your head, Michael."

If I spend less time in my head than where am I spending the rest?

"Good question my student! That would mean spending more time in your heart."

Would that be because it's closer to my spirit?

"Yes, Michael! Your heart is a lot closer to your real self. The person you are not is in your head," Tom replied. "If people only spent more time listening to their hearts instead of their heads than their true expressions would rain down on the world. The cornerstones of their lives would remain balanced because people would understand the necessity of what truly matters. That comes when you listen to your heart. You will live a life that you designed."

Instead of fabricating your existence in the ways that others would have liked you too.

"That is how you re-establish the connection between your real self and the physical world. Just change vehicles, Michael. Get out of your head and into your heart!"

Let my true potential reveal itself to the planet! I said.

"The heart can reveal who you really are. And when it does people will see the real Michael Jamieson," Tom replied.

It sounds better than running after the tireless images of my mind that so far haven't given me any sense of happiness.

"The reality of it is that the wants and desires of your ego are never satisfied. You can never have enough and therefore you can never be happy with a life of always wanting more stuff."

I can see that living this way is a choice, I said to Tom.

"No Michael! Living in your heart and balancing your life journey has nothing to do with choices."

No!

"It is a consciousness! You just have to see it first. Than you can embrace it."

Tom broke stride from our rather lengthy walk down the brown sandy beach explaining that he had to meet with his next client. He explained that the purpose of our visit that day was a way for him to open my eyes to the world we live in and the beings we truly are. A method to show me that money, material and possessions are only creations of the ego-mind in conjunction with the ideals of the physical world.

It was an awakening for me to realize that each and every human being is in actuality the same. An information overload so to speak! And Tom mentioned that I would have a ton of information to sift through after our talks together. No doubt he was right! However, he wanted me to spend less time thinking in my head and more time listening to my heart when it came to making sense of it all. And from that day I shifted the process as best I could from my head to my heart.

The fact of the matter was that afternoon I was the person Tom was generalizing about when he mentioned the world living out of balance, from the confines of their egoic head. Tom the crazy surfer dude obliterated a mighty chip that sat atop my shoulder. The one overshadowing my ability to see the real world! In a few short hours Tom told the tale of my life in an indirect yet applicable fashion.

As I made my way back to the center I was angry with myself because I couldn't see the things that Tom had pointed out until today. Thinking how different my life would have been if I could have seen them before all of the most chaotic events.

In a state of disappointed awe I shunned the powers of my mind for the time being making note of the footprints my steps were forming in the sand. I believed from that point onward they represented a metaphor marking the next path on my journey in life. In fact, they molded the "First Day in May" as the day that my life would change for the better.

Reflection

"...All you behold; tho it appears Without, it is Within, in your imagination,
of which this World of Mortality is but a shadow."
-William Blake-

Growing up in a military family meant one thing for sure! It meant that my family and I were certain to visit a great number of places in a short period of time. My father was a servant to his country. A career solider of sorts! In fact, he was a decorated navy seal who spent time in active duty in Korea, Vietnam, Kuwait and Somalia. On numerous occasions my father was offered the opportunity through his official rank to escape the battlegrounds for the confines of a cushy office but his passion for combat kept him fighting.

Following Vietnam, my father was given a high profile, special operations command post stationed out of Hawaii. All we knew of his latest position was that the job was high security, classified. Apparently, he had twelve elite soldiers under his command that at the drop of a hat could be running off on top-secret missions around the globe.

As a kid, Hawaii was a great backdrop to grow up. I mean who wouldn't love the chance to explore the lush rainforests, the ancient volcano craters and the big surf. It was a vast place for exploration and adventure. It was also my first brush with the experience of death.

Looking back, I remembered my brother and I had a secret hang out on the north side of Honolulu. A beautiful inlet beach! Accessible only by way of a short hike through the jungle. Isolated from tourists and less frequented by locals it was a safe haven to seek refuge from the pressures of being a kid. Emerging from the trees you were met with the big blue ocean crashing against the towering cliffs that surrounded the inlet. My brother and I would spend hours playing in the surf and sand just being crazy kids.

The cliff borders stretched from the outer perimeter of the inlet forming mostly a shelter for the quiet volcanic beach. Wide open, treeless and unprotected, the cliffs appeared to us as mountains looking down on the rest of the world. It was here that we exercised most of our childish yet fearless imagination.

On most days it was approximately a ten foot drop from the ridge face to the water below our favorite location. Unless of course, the raging surf gods decided otherwise. On many occasions we would just sit with our legs dangling over the edge of the rocks contemplating life as the waves crashed below. However, one afternoon we had an awful lot to contemplate on the subject of life and even death.

My brother was given a camera for his birthday a couple of days previous to our visit to the cliffs. As an inquisitive little kid he wanted to shoot images of everything under the sun. Whether it was people, places or things he wanted to be able to capture it all on film.

At the beach that day he saw a fisherman at the far end of the cliff with a setting sun in the distance. He decided it would be a great image to catch. So he drew his camera from the sack on his shoulders and went in search of a position on the Cliffside to take the shot. However, being totally consumed with the task at hand he was unaware that the surf on our side of the ridge was raging. As it crashed against the rock face it sprayed a continuous mist of water everywhere.

My brother saw only the picture he was trying to capture. And in an instant all I remember hearing was the force of a colossal wave exploding on the rocks and my brother vanishing from the spot where he previously stood. There were no sounds other than the noise of the wind and ocean. Other than the original elements any additional noise was completely drowned out. Where had my brother gone I wondered as I scanned the area for his presence? I remember screaming his name only to hear it blow back at me with the force of the hurling sea. In bewilderment, I approached the cliffs edge to look at the waters surface some ten feet below. It was in that moment that I witnessed the harsh reality of my brother clinging to a series of rocks below in increasingly forceful surf. I knew that he was a strong swimmer but too small in fact a frame to battle with the size of these waves. His strength was certain to be limited as he fought for his life and there wouldn't be much time before he was battered against the rocks guarding the shoreline.

So without formulating any type of emergency plan I shouted to my brother whom I realized couldn't hear me. I could see that his efforts were being placed in the struggle that had ensued. In desperation, I remembered the fisherman so I screamed in the direction of his location some 100 yards away. In fact, I began waving my arms and jumping up and down at the same time hoping to muster a response. As I continued to look as though I was attempting to flag a landing plane I couldn't be sure that the fisherman even knew I was there. So instead of waiting around long enough to find out I thrust myself off the rocks above with the purpose of rescuing my brother who was in serious danger.

My actions only proved to be pointless and I should have known better. The intentions I had were good but the assessment of the situation was poor. At that time the waters pull was extremely forceful increasing with power each and every second we were in the water. There was no conceivable way we could swim out of the predicament. I had miscalculated the scenario and as a result placed us both in the hands of danger. The only mode of survival was to cling to a rock twenty feet or so offshore away from the piercing rocks that protected the cliff face. In my mind I kept trying to formulate an escape route. It was clear in my head because I repeatedly saw myself swimming to safety. However, physically we hung on tiring to the point of exhaustion, certain to be crushed on the rocks in due time. That is all I could remember. The battle. The fighting. The struggle for our young lives!

During the event I remembered blacking out. As I awoke I remember squinting due to the bright light that blinded my eyes. My brother was beside me. We were no longer clinging to the rocks offshore. Exhausted, I inquired aloud as to what had happened. Much to my surprise the answers didn't come from my brother. It was the fisherman that responded. That day was my first stare down with death. My brother and I were spared by the kindness of the heavens in calling upon a neighboring guardian. Looking up at the fisherman I managed to muster a thank you. I was indeed grateful to him for saving us from the potential tragedy that could have resulted. He was someone I would never forget as long as I would live.

My brother and I made a pact following that day's unexpected events. We decided that we would never mention our brush with near death to anyone, especially mom and dad. We understood the ramifications that their knowledge of the ordeal would bring. Our safe haven would be gone simply due to the fact that they would never allow us to venture there again on our own. To the important place that my brother and I had grown to cherish during our time in Hawaii! It was the escape we needed from the troubles of life. A place we could make time stand still.

I am not sure if the experience changed us or not. We were still fearless kids following the near disaster. Perhaps it even fueled the thoughts of immortality that most children seem to have. After all, most of us truly believe we will live forever!

In the days preceding the incident I remember returning to our sanctuary, perched atop the cliffs overlooking the ocean. I turned to my brother asking if he had died that day what would he want to come back to life as next? In that moment he smiled at me remaining speechless. After a few moments of silence he stated someone like me. There was no doubt in my mind the event made a huge impact on the life of my brother. It truly brought our relationship closer together. On the other hand for myself, the magnitude of the drama stood still in my mind. The jury was still out on the effects it had for better or worse in relation to my life journey. But at least it had me thinking!

Chapter Seven:
The Second Day in May:
Our Place in the World

"In those moments when we forget ourselves—not thinking,
"Am I happy?" but completely oblivious to our little ego—
we spend a brief but beautiful holiday in heaven.
-Eknath Easwaran-

In the days since my last encounter with Tom the "Life Coach" I spent a great deal of time focusing on myself as a spiritual entity in the physical world. During these moments I didn't have time to continue my contemplation of "why me" or "poor me." In fact, I learned from Tom that life isn't even about me anyway. Essentially, I was trying to get over myself—my ego. Something that wouldn't prove to be an easy task! After all my already hefty sense of self had been blocking my true views of the world for almost all of my entire adult life. In fact, I was left questioning my real place in life. Something other than the sense of self-importance that my ego had misled me to believe!

The second day in May had arrived for Tom and I. It signified another day spent searching for the lost answers to my life. He was someone I was growing fond of. And I believe it was his vision and insight that left me yearning to know more. After all, he had opened the door to a whole new world for me. So as valuable as the other days were at the center in my trek back to a healthy life, I grew to the point that the only days that mattered were the days in May that I was able to further my personal development under the guidance of Tom.

As I hiked down to the beach that day I could see Tom skipping rocks off the crystal clear water in front of him. The day was yet again sunny and warm without any hint of wind.

"Welcome back, my student."

Thank You, I replied.

"Have you digested the information from our last meeting or are you still regurgitating it?"

I would definitely lean to the regurgitation end of it, Tom.

"Very well! I would totally expect that."

So what is on tap for today? I asked him.

"Michael, now that you have some insight as to what you are we can move on to exploring why you are here in this physical place."

Why I am here? That is something that I have been thinking about also.

"So have you come up with any answers?"

Before, I would have said that I was here to ascend on fame and fortune but as I begin to see life differently I believe that would be all to shallow a response.

"I commend you on that realization."

I have a feeling that we are here on the planet to give it something it needs.

"You are correct, Michael. Now knowing what you truly are you have the capacity to see that you are here for something beyond any self-serving nature."

Before I never would have admitted that. However, I honestly see it differently!

"Okay, so your myopic views of the world are shifting as we speak, Michael."

I am not sure what you are getting at?

"Well, let's start small and work toward the bigger picture, shall we, Michael," Tom shouted in excitement.

I can do that!

"Michael, what are you looking for in life?"

I can honestly say that I have been a little lost in that department.

"So lets get back on track!"

There is a huge void in my life! Happiness is something that has been eluding me for years. I have been so busy stalking stardom. You know the money, the fame, the notoriety and the success but it seems that I am never satisfied with that. In the process I sacrificed my home life, my family, friends and loved ones. The relentless pursuit of excellence created a constant state of turmoil inside of me. A destructive force I guess.

"So where does that lead you in terms of what you are searching for in life?" Tom asked again.

I would have to say that I want the important things back. Like my wife, my daughter, my friends and my family!

"Correct me if I am wrong with the summarization, Michael!"

Fire away!

"It appears to me that you have been chasing possessions your entire life. The job, money, material, fame, success, family, friends, reputation and titles."

That is absolutely a fair synopsis, I replied.

"You must understand that in chasing possessions there attainment doesn't bring you closer to the answers you are in search of."

Let me guess! The pursuit of these objects is the insecurity of the ego.

Tom smiled. "No question the sense of importance in attaining these possessions comes from the ego's image created in your mind."

So what is the alternative to chasing after perceived success? I asked.

"You need to stop the pursuit and initiate the interpretation of the answers that already exist inside of you."

So you believe the answers are already there? I questioned Tom.

"Michael, you are looking for answers to direct your life in the attainment of the possessions that most of our society feels hold unquestionable importance."

And that is how the ego tricks us?

"Living in your head encompasses the knowledge of experience and there is nothing wrong with that but it is not the true wisdom that reigns free in your heart."

Interesting! I said dumbfounded by Tom's account.

"The way I have interpreted your life of recent has been by listening to your building of a tower with the purpose of getting closer to god."

Closer to god! I said unsure of the point Tom was trying to make.

Tom pointed to the sky. "Yes, Michael. By compiling a collection of possessions you unconsciously believe you are building a stairway to heaven where you will find the answers that will direct you to what it is you are searching for."

So that is what you mean by building a tower to reach god?

"Yes! The problem is that you haven't been able to see that the answers you are in search of are already inside of you."

They are?

Tom smiled directing a tightly closed fist over his heart. "They lie within your heart, Michael! Start by listening to your heart and you will begin to know enough to follow it."

And where will that take me? I asked.

"When you are finally able to accomplish the method of listening to your heart you will know you are in the right place in the journey called life."

You mean I will stop chasing objects without meaning?

"I wouldn't say that your wife and daughter are objects that lack meaning, Michael."

No, I guess they have a great deal of meaning to me!

"That is why you want them back so badly."

I suppose your right!

"However, to get your life direction on the right track you need to start looking at your life from a different perspective."

You mean ending the pursuit of possessions!

"Stop chasing possessions on the outside and start looking for the answers on the inside," Tom sparked.

I had to take a moment to myself. That meant breaking from the conversation for the time being to recover from the immense blow delivered to my ego from Tom's realistic assessment of my life.

"Let me ask you a question, Michael. What is it that people like teachers, police officers, lawyers, financial advisors, doctors and bankers do in their daily lives?"

Well, I guess they offer help and advice regarding their professional expertise. Where are you going with the question? I asked in a perturbed tone of voice.

"Look deeper at the roles these people play in our lives, Michael."

I already answered the question! I said sharply.

"To some extent you have given me the answer you want me to hear but I don't think you see it just yet yourself," Tom replied.

I already told you that these professions offer help, service, advice and protection.

"So what is it that these people and people in general actually do?"

It's a job, I stated.

"No, it is a whole lot more," Tom replied.

Than what is it?

"When you sit in your office in San Francisco analyzing the stock market everyday whom are you doing that for?"

My career. My boss. The investors. All because I enjoy what it is I am doing.

"Why? Michael."

I am able to give advice, guidance and aid to those who need it most.

"You just mentioned the word "give" in your last sentence."

So giving is what all of the people we are talking about do in life?

"You said it! Giving! That is what every single human being on the planet does during their time on earth whether they actually recognize it or not."

So what?

Tom took a serious tone. "So what! Not only are we all made up of the same energy but we are also carrying the one common goal that drives our existence. To give of yourself to others! In fact, to give to the world, Michael."

Giving? I am completely confused.

"Sure. Everyone from a policeman to a waitress does one thing and one thing only. They give of themselves. They serve their communities through their roles. You do it also, Mr. Jamieson. You just don't realize it yet."

I have to admit I see your point but I never really looked at it that way before.

"Of course you didn't, Michael. If you saw the same world that I did we wouldn't be having today's conversation."

I see how adults give of themselves through the various roles they assume in their communities but how does that apply to children and animals for instance? I questioned.

"You're not quite seeing the overall theme of a life of giving of your inner power," Tom replied. "Michael, whether its family, children or your spouse they all provide the same thing. Just like a dog or a cat!"

So what do they give?

"The problem is that you are attempting to quantify the gift that these energies are offering to the universe while they are in it. You simply cannot view it that way."

So what is the missing link here, Tom?

"Remember it has nothing to do with training, education, titles or designations! We are a part of the universe to express our own inner energy to the world."

Okay, I remember that part!

"All everyone truly does is give from the heart, Michael."

It must be more complex than just that, I replied.

"Your right. The complexity lies in the fact that most people are unconscious to their real purpose in life."

And that is to give? I asked.

"Correct! Giving is all we can do while we are alive in the physical sense. I should say that giving is the only thing that is real because it comes from the place that is real, from the heart."

I guess my view of giving has always been as a means to receive something in return, I responded.

"I hope you now recognize the power of the ego with that idea, Michael. That is how you wind up centering yourself."

I do! However, giving is one thing but what about our own survival?

"Your innate power. Your spirit, Michael, was put in your physical body for one reason."

And what could that be?

"Its in there to give a piece of yourself to the world in making it a better place," Tom mentioned.

How can I do that? "Whether it is the directions you offer a lost stranger, business advice to clients, making someone smile during a difficult time or donating yourself to those in need."

It certainly encompasses a whole spectrum of situations.

"Michael, society has learned from generations before them a scarcity consciousness."

A scarcity consciousness? I questioned.

"People have learned that you must succeed to be able to provide for yourself and your family! We have become entrenched in running from perceived failure. However, in attempting to out run the very thing we are trying to avoid we make it our focus. That focus of never having enough becomes a consciousness for many and hence a lifestyle where we fear for our survival."

I see your point. The ego at work!

"All you have that is real in the world is the powerful spirit that rests beyond the confines of your outer body and its numerous parts. It is your god given destiny to express that power through the eight cornerstones with the purpose of making a difference in the world before you leave it."

So where does the scarcity component fit in, I asked.

"When your mind fills you with the need for more on a constant level. It misleads you because it fears never having enough. What the ego doesn't understand is that when you give of yourself from the heart, your real inner spirit, it truly makes a difference in your life. Your offering to the world encourages the universe to provide you with everything you will need to survive."

It does? I said.

"Closing your fist by clinging firmly to everything you have instead of giving with an open hand will indefinitely delay the true meaning of your own personal journey."

How so?

"Michael, by opening your hand and your heart you are relinquishing the power of the mind that places self-importance in such things as the need for money, titles, material items and having more."

So I embrace the idea that we are all united through the energy of the universe. The perfection? I stated.

"In doing so you become closer to the wealth that a perfect world has to offer you in return for the wealth that you express to others," Tom replied.

So it's not about giving with the expectation of receiving?

Tom managed a smile. "Not at all, Michael! Scour the history books and examine the many people who defined a life through giving. By their making a difference in the world they were provided with the abundance of the universe in return. A source of riches like no other."

I can see the "take, take, take" mentality that the world has employed.

"The universe is in perfect balance. It rewards your giving with the abundance that you were meant to have in your life."

"Michael, the millions of dollars you make, the big mansion you live in and the fancy cars you drive don't make you a better human being. In fact, they don't even begin to define who you truly are."

I am not so sure they make you happy either, I stated.

"You cannot take them with you when you leave the physical world."

I guess they are just rentals until we die?

"So all you can truly do to honor yourself is halt the endless pursuit of the answers that we know already lie within," Tom mentioned.

So it appears that I have been missing out on something truly amazing. We should be giving away pieces of ourselves to serve others.

"There is nothing wrong with wanting the finer things in life, Michael," Tom remarked.

Oh! Isn't that a contradiction to what we have been discussing, I said.

"Not if you understand that they are just things that really don't matter in life," Tom replied.

You mean items to simply have fun with but not to get obsessed about.

"The ego makes possessions an obsession for most people."

So if we understand the real value and meaning in them than we won't succumb to the sacrifice of our true selves in enjoying them.

"Fun items can certainly motivate your cause in life. They can be the get up and go that you sometimes need in the morning. Most times the cause as you are coming to understand in life, our lesson today, is enough to fuel your desire. However, rewards from the universe if left in context with the appropriate meaning and value can be enjoyed while you are here."

As long as we don't let them define whom we actually are, I said.

"You just need to establish the foundation from your heart instead of with the mind," Tom replied.

So living in my head links me to the expectations of others and is guided by my ego.

"Yes, you are right, Michael."

So my purpose thus far has been distorted by my selfish focus for my own advancement in the world.

"Right again!" Tom stated.

I am starting to understand the picture from the heart we've been discussing today.

"These aren't images, Michael. It is reality. The truth," Tom replied.

The truth?

"The only truth that exists, Michael. That is to just be yourself!"

How could I forget that part!

"Living from the heart gives you a sense of purpose as to why you are here."

You mean giving and serving?

"Yes! Giving, serving and helping from the heart is wrapped in love. All things that come from the heart are the same things that reside there. Made from the same pure ingredients that comprise your true self. Your purpose in life."

The same purity that cannot be overshadowed by an uncontrollable ego! I said.

"Now you have it, Michael!" Tom shouted in agreement.

I guess we have to keep life in perspective?

"Absolutely! You will have much more of an appreciation for life when you live it from the heart instead of the material motives centered around your mind."

It makes complete sense!

"Come with me," Tom said.

Off we went walking down the endless beach of Monterey. There was no telling what was still left in the time ahead with Tom. In fact, I was never one to be in the moment so to speak. Usually, ten steps ahead of myself and everyone else for that matter! Too jaded to witness any of the perceived beauty that the planet had to offer. Spending time outside was something that I'd always cherished growing up but also something I traded in for the cherry wood panels of an executive office in the financial district. It was truly great to absorb myself in the astonishing world of Tom's outer office. The powder blue sky, the salty sea air and the sounds of barking sea lions basking in the sun, frolicking in the surf nearby!

"Something we haven't yet focused on today is balance," Tom mentioned.

You mean the eight cornerstones we express our lives from, I replied.

"Remember, how we express our inner power?"

I sure do!

"As much as we express ourselves in the eight cornerstones we also have to realize we were created to give equally amongst them."

I can see the motto! Live to Give, I remarked.

"Again, when your living from your heart you are giving of yourself. The true purpose that exists within becomes spread to the areas that honestly matter. In all eight cornerstones you give equally the energy that comprises who and what you are to lead you to a balanced yet abundant life."

In your head, you are blinded into seeing only one or two of the cornerstones as a priority, I reiterated.

Tom raised both his arms in victory. "A prodigy you have become, Michael. It relates back to how you see the world you physically live in. We know that our only purpose is to give as much of ourselves as we can."

It is also clear that it is the only real truth in the world, I stated.

"In the eight cornerstones that we express ourselves in, we can only give. Whether it is to our profession, social, mental, financial, personal or spiritual. We express here, we give here and we live here."

And this is why you're here—to make a difference not only in your life experience but also to the physical world in these eight areas?

"That is why you are here, Michael," Tom replied.

The spirit coming to fruition! I remarked.

"From the heart! It's a balance amongst living and giving. A connection to what is really important."

I have learned a lot, without a doubt, I admitted.

"Once again, Michael, you already had the answers inside of you. You just weren't conscious of it."

I looked at Tom in surprise. How so?

"We all know the truth but we just fail to follow it. It boils down to whether or not we acknowledge it. Whether it becomes conscious or unconscious most of it is buried inside waiting to come out."

I assume most of it is clouded in the unconscious realm?

"True! It is easier to blame others. The circumstances. The situations we have experienced for losing our direction in life," Tom replied.

You have described my life to a tee, Tom, I said.

"I know Michael! That pretty much describes all of us at one point or another. It requires great courage to take responsibility for what and who you have become. And when you finally realize that you will be living from a consciousness that you have never seen before. A medium of power that can change your life and thus your entire experience."

My eyes have been opening further and further every minute of our discussion, I admitted.

"You will get there," Tom replied. "It is another stop on your continuous journey through life. All we have to do is just keep you in the moment for you to witness the incredible power."

Tom glanced at his watch during our conversation and I knew it meant that the second day in May was coming to a close. In that instant my consciousness became awakened in relation to my life both past and present. For almost all of my physical existence I realized I had been living in a fog of unconsciousness. Allowing people, places and things to dictate my path instead of captaining my own. Trapped in my head. Held hostage by my flourishing ego. Ignorant of my heart!

Suddenly, it was all falling into perspective. The dark cloud may have been mobilizing from its position over my head. Was it finally lifting? Or had my consciousness made a push to open the door?

Whatever it was I was actually beginning to see my life shifting in a different direction. I think I was taking a deeper look inside during that moment. Spending less time focusing on myself. For the first time I could see the pattern that Tom had been trying to emphasize along the way. Above, Down, Inside, Out was the direction of my energy connection. I was finally catching on but I was skeptical at how Tom had made it all sound so easy to transform.

Reflection

"It is the mind that maketh good or ill,
that maketh wretch or happy, rich or poor."
-Edmund Spencer-

My brother and I had a bond that most family members never share in a lifetime. We were very different people despite the distinct connection we had with one another. You see I was the analytical one. The one who would have to deliberate for a lengthy period over the life and death scenarios before choosing to parachute out of a burning plane. My brother on the other hand just followed his heart and would jump from the same plane without even a second thought. He was fearless in my eyes and he even taught me at times to live from the heart. However, as we neared adulthood the gap in differences between us became more evident. Only one of us for sure remained fearless and that wasn't myself. It was ultimately my brother that I could honestly say was very much alive in his experience of life.

I use to call my brother crazy and sometimes even stupid. He was the same kid who surfed amongst the killer waves on the North Shore of Oahu. He free climbed rock faces around the globe and even went diving in the presence of great white sharks. The things I looked at and saw fear were the same things he looked at and saw amazement.

As kids it started when my brother would unknowingly catch poisonous snakes in the desert of Arizona. He would eat live insects on a dare, ask out the most beautiful girls with the largest of boyfriends, and visit the principal's office for discipline only to tell him what he thought needed to be done to improve the school. He was the brother I loved, the same brother whose fearless acts ended up costing him his life before he reached maturity.

He was eighteen years of age looking forward to embarking on a journey traveling the globe. I on the other hand was readying myself for the experience of an Ivey league education. Once again, we followed our hearts in different directions. With his backpack in his hand and my Ivey league scholarship in mine our lives were about to carry us into new and exciting worlds. Although, our paths would be certain to cross the directions would fail to be the ones that appeared most obvious. It was the birth of a terrifying incident that would forever change our relationship before the newest journey could take place.

I remembered the terrifying event like it happened yesterday. It was two weeks before I was leaving for college that I arrived home from my summer job to find my brother horsing around with my father's .22-magnum pistol in the backyard of the house.

I could not begin to describe the horror I felt as I watched him point the weapon he commanded towards numerous objects pretending to shoot them aimlessly. During that time I openly chastised him for his ridiculous behavior. It was dangerous, immature and irresponsible. However, like always he assured me the gun wasn't loaded. That everything was okay. And as usual me being the uptight of the two I found calm in his reassurance. But the second he motioned to prove his point he directly pointed the weapon towards his forehead. In that instant he pulled the trigger only to unveil the tortuous thunder that I will never forget for the rest of my life. My brother collapsed instantly making a sudden free fall to the same ground where seconds ago he stood.

At first, I recalled screaming the word "No" from the top of my lungs but he was never one to listen to anything that his older brother had to say. After witnessing the event I rushed to dial 911. In doing so I remembered him constantly calling me conservative, the reserved one, and never any fun. And he wasn't altogether wrong. No doubt I was a little fearful! Perhaps even a bit cautious with my life. However, in that moment I was undeniably scared. But not for my life! I was speechless as I looked on in shock, as my brother lay motionless in a dark pool of his own blood. My heart was racing at a thousand times its regular speed. I knew beyond any shadow of a doubt that my brother was gone. At eighteen years of age he had chosen a different path in life. It was an unforgettable eighteen years for him but a not so forgivable time for me.

Try informing your parents that your kid brother shot himself in the head while screwing around with what he thought was an unarmed revolver in your own backyard.

They were shocked at the news. In fact, it was my brother's death that challenged our family unity in the years to come. The death unraveled my father. On the spot he retired from the world of violence that he devoted almost all of his entire life towards.

Not only did my family change without the brother I loved but my parents found a means to blame me for his own reckless behavior. That's right! They decided amidst all of the turmoil that they would hold me responsible for his death. Me! The older, wiser and smarter one of the two apparently should have been able to prevent such an accident from happening. For leaving so easily I was never able to forgive my brother. Quite simply because he had left me behind to experience the destruction of our family! The same family that placed the entire responsibility for his death on my maturing shoulders!

When I left for the mainland I carried a heavy heart with me. We buried my brother in California where he was born before I enrolled at college. Upon entering my freshman year I started to put the past behind me the best I could. One of the ways I accomplished that task was to separate from any regular contact with my parents. I didn't return phone calls. I spent holidays on my own. Sure, there were times when they'd call me to inquire into my life at school. However, I remained distant in our conversations, which I am sure they took note of.

After all, I knew in their eyes that they held me responsible for the death of my brother. They never let me forget it. And that was something that they surely must have acknowledged doing along the way. It was toxic for me to continue living with the blame. They began to punish me for it by attempting to control my life from afar. However, it wasn't easy for them to force me into decisions I didn't want to go along with from a different time zone. They even made attempts at threatening to pull their financial support of my education. I often thought one son is already gone! Did they actually want to ruin the life of the one they had left?

Once I learned that their support was purely conditional I emotionally dissolved the connection with my parents. Forgiving them so to speak. It was really the only choice. Talking it out didn't work. And in the end their influence almost had me believe that there was some truth to the fact that I could have prevented my brother's death. In the time that we grew apart as a family I never forgave my brother for handing me the gun after he ultimately used it to kill himself. Metaphorically so to speak, I accepted that I was holding his smoking gun. I was on trial for his death. For the mistake that he made! And for that I carried around a phenomenal suitcase full of emotions. In that time I found it incredibly difficult to forgive myself for the accident. And I didn't!

Chapter Eight:
The Third Day in May:
Forget the Forgiveness

"The man who never alters his opinion is like
standing water and breeds reptiles of the mind."
-William Blake-

As I was awake battling the cosmic storm of thoughts parading through my mind I motioned to catch a glimpse of the alarm clock beside my bed. In big, red and bold letters it displayed 4:30 a.m. The morning surf was booming as it crashed on the beach in the distance. It was all I had to disrupt me from the blame I had immersed myself in surrounding the near destruction of my life.

I was slowly coming to understand what I had learned from Tom in our meetings. The incredible inner power that is us and its important purpose in life. However, amidst the acknowledgement of the truth I started to doubt my ability to connect with it. Quite honestly because I carried around a hefty resentment for the things that I had done in the past!

For starters, I still held anger towards my parents for blaming me for the death of my brother years ago. Something I guess inside I had believed I had forgiven them for. But even after removing any and all communications from their toxicity they too still had a method of punishing me. A method far greater than they even knew! It was the guilt, the blame and the shame that I imposed upon myself for what they believed I could have stopped. A punishment I suffered then and most certainly held on to now.

I despised my brother for leaving the way he did. Almost knowingly placing the responsibility on me. Something he always did when he was alive. It was hard to imagine loving and hating a person so much at the same time. However, that is how I felt. I forgave him for dying but resented him for ruining my relationship with our parents.

Most of the aspects of my life for which I held contempt for didn't hold a candle to the hatred I had for myself. More than ever I was consumed with anger and I had constant reminders of it daily. A blizzard of internal conflict resided in my drug dependent body. Everything from the resentment of my brother, the behavior of my parents, my failed marriage, the drugs, the lies, the infatuation with success! I resented it all. Angry at myself for watching my life plummet into the depths of despair! I just wanted to rot away because I felt that it was the only thing I deserved. I was intensely unhappy and I hated my life.

Suddenly, over the intercom system in my room I was interrupted by a familiar voice. "Michael, you there?" It said.

It was Tom. Yes, I am awake, I answered in a lowly tone.

"Meet me in the lobby in about 10 minutes, alright," Tom requested.

No problem, I replied.

I couldn't help but wonder what Tom's early morning call was all about. However, after everything I had encountered up to that point during my stay at the center I had a feeling that it had some important meaning behind it.

As I entered the lobby it was dead silent. Only Louisa was present, looking as though she was preparing for another day. Then the silence was met with a large roar as Tom entered the picture.

"Good morning, everyone," He shouted upon entering the lobby.

Tom was outfitted in a blackish-gray wet suit and appeared to be holding two surfboard's in his grasp.

"You haven't forgot how to shred have you?" He asked me.

It has been awhile!

"It's like learning to ride a bike, Michael. You never forget," Tom said with a loud laugh that echoed through the cathedral halls of the center. "The surf this morning is unbelievable, Michael."

I would hope so based on the way it's crashing on the beach! So is that the reason you rang me this morning. To hit the beach?

"What you're about to witness is truly amazing. So I thought you wouldn't mind substituting a little surfing for your regular fitness session, Michael."

No problem with that. Last time I checked surfing was still a sport!

"Well than! If there aren't any further complaints with my choice of activities, lets hit the beach," Tom yelled as he motioned for the door.

Off we went into the darkness of the early morning. As we arrived on the sandy shores the waves roared in the distance. It was rough and loud as the surf crashed on the breaking point just offshore.

"Here is a wet suit I brought for you, Michael," Tom stated as he tossed it in my general direction.

I assume the water is a little chilly this time of year, Tom?

"Lets just say it isn't quite seasonal," Tom replied.

While I got situated in my suit the sun unveiled a parallel line of deep orange through the darkness on the edge of the horizon.

"I'll meet you out there," Tom shouted through the gusty wind. "You absolutely do not want to miss out on the sunrise, Michael," He yelled.

As we paddled out we both sat on our surfboards in amazement of the sun beginning to awaken to the new day.

"I felt your energy this morning, Michael."

How so? I asked him.

"I understand that you are experiencing a great deal of inner conflict regarding the person you have become and the life you have been leading."

How do you know that?

"Its not that hard, Michael. I have been in your shoes my friend. The internal conflict, the torture, the doubt and your mindset are all products of the fear laced ego at work."

I suppose you are right. However, it seems as though it has always gotten the best of me. I have to be honest! There have been many moments of late where I have wanted to just pack it in. To give up!

"Listen, Michael. I have tried to forgive not only myself but the people in my life for what has happened, just like you! However, constantly reminding yourself of it 24/7 isn't going to help."

Do you have any suggestions, Tom?

"You bet I do! First, you have to remember that you have been through some incredibly powerful ordeals, Michael. Events and experiences that would have crushed many a man before you! But not Mr. Michael Jamieson. Not You!"

Why do you suppose I survived? I asked Tom.

"It certainly says a lot about who you really are, Michael."

I managed to hide a smile in the darkness with the words that Tom had uttered in kindness. However, in a flash I watched Tom as he paddled out to catch what seemed like a colossal wave. The surf was full of force, but not enough to silence the cheer of Tom shouting and screaming as he tamed a wild wave.

Next, it was my turn to share in his exhilaration for Mother Nature! I reeled in a heavy counterpart in succession to that of Tom's. A little rusty I did my best to keep my balance. However, my conditioning showed and I was sucked up by the mighty tides.

"Pretty awesome wouldn't you say, Michael? Tom yelled.

That was amazing!

"When was the last time you felt like you do right now? Tom asked me.

I can honestly say it has been years! I replied. Unless of course you want to include drug related effects.

"Surfing is very soulful, Michael," Tom remarked.

How so?

"No better way to introduce the energy inside of you to the power of the universe than right here, right now!" Tom shouted.

I see your point!

"Look Michael!" Tom said in a serious tone. "You are working through the major motion pictures of the past inside of your head. Reliving the moments all over again. The actions, your responses and the outcomes."

I am attempting to accept what has happened and to forgive the involved parties instead of punishing them and myself.

"So how has that been going for you?" Tom asked.

Not so well I am afraid.

"Forgiveness will not work in your life, Michael!"

That seems like a contentious statement! I mentioned to him.

"You hear a lot about forgiveness these days, Michael. Being able to forgive people for their words, actions and behaviors. Even the idea of forgiving yourself!"

So what is wrong with being able to let go of the turmoil that rests upon ones life? I asked.

"You just mentioned letting go of how people and even you have expressed your life towards others."

I did? I stated in surprise. So what?

"How have you been using the tool of forgiveness up to now in your life, Michael?"

I am not sure what you mean? I said in confusion.

"Have you truly been able to forgive yourself for the death of your brother?

How about the parents who blame you for the accident? What about your decision to leave Lisa and your daughter? And even the drug addiction you developed that nearly cost you your life?"

Okay, I get the point! That's enough! I interrupted sharply.

"I know you sit awake at night in your room wishing you had done things differently."

I ask "What if?" an awful lot.

"Is it all helping you forgive, Michael?"

I am not really sure how to answer that question, I replied.

"Forgiveness, the way I see it is used in the physical realm as a means to hang on to the resentment we hold for either ourselves or others," Tom said.

Well, that pretty much sums up what I have been participating in!

"Forgiveness is a term and a method we use to attract negative feelings to what we continue to harbor. In the end we carry it and use it to bring up the resentment that consumes us later under different situations, instances and circumstances."

Sort of like that old quote I remember: "We forgive, but never forget."

"Absolutely, Michael!"

So as I have immersed myself in the negative events of my past you are telling me I haven't been able to let go of the second-guessing I have been harboring?

"You can call it second-guessing, pain, resentment, anger, fear or whatever. But they all come from your attempts to forgive others and yourself."

I see!

"Tell me, Michael, have you been able to fully let go of the things creating internal conflict?"

No, I haven't at all. They are burning in my gut with great guilt now more than ever.

Again, Tom had managed to chip away at the protective layer that surrounded my narrow view of the life I was leading. As I watched him venture in the direction of another wave I became consciously aware that I spent countless hours masking my internal thoughts, feelings and emotions with the illusion of forgiveness. A tool that enabled me to relive the past! In addition, crippling me with the storage of the events, my judgments and resentment. Allowing me the opportunity to unleash its negativity whenever I deemed appropriate.

"You see, forgiveness has a hold on you right now, Michael, because it constantly plays out the events in your head. In fact, most people hold these things over themselves or the heads of others down the road."

I shook my head in frustration. Your right! We tend to remind others of these events when they least expect it.

"How many times have you heard of someone making a mistake in a marriage only to have a loved one for instance constantly remind him/her of it during every disagreement after that?"

It doesn't present itself as an empowering experience.

"That's because its not," Tom replied.

Tom turned to stare directly into my eyes. "Michael, you can choose to see the world as it truly is or how your mind believes it is! You can actually see the perfection that exists in the universe and understand that you don't need forgiveness to resolve the past."

Than what do I need to do to solve my contempt?

"Go back to the quote you mentioned earlier."

A light bulb switched on in my mind. "We forgive but we never forget". I paused in thought to contemplate the quote and it hit me. We should just forget?

"How long ago did all the events that you are constantly replaying over and over in your mind take place, Michael?"

I guess it ranges from a very long time to within the past couple of weeks, I replied.

"So what does that represent, Michael?"

I would say the past, I responded.

"So why not forget it? You certainly cannot change what has already happened! So what good is it going to do you in constantly revisiting it? Punishing yourself and the others for the events that have previously occurred?"

I suppose if I just learned to forget I could go on without harboring the negativity that I have been carrying around, regurgitating all of the time.

"Remember that, Michael."

I have to admit that I have been sleepwalking through life. I stated out loud.

"The past is a movie that has already had its time in the theater. You cannot change it. It makes no sense punishing anyone, you included, for what has already happened. As a result all you are doing is stunting your present growth as a person."

I see what you mean when you mentioned keeping me in the moment!

We paused our conversation for a brief time. Sitting side by side on our surfboards amidst the voluminous waves gazing at the bright orange hue of the horizon as a full sunrise illuminated the darkness. Metaphorically, for me it was as if a light was being cast upon the darkness of my former life. Taking it from hopeless to hopeful. And I had Tom to thank for that.

I can understand that I have been obsessed with living from my head.

"Michael, never forget that the universe is perfectly balanced."

I know! It just depends on how you view it. But I guess it is all in perfect balance.

"The balance in the universe is the same perfection that should be incorporated into letting the world see your real self."

I agree with you, Tom!

"The mind makes decisions. The heart makes commitments!" Tom stated. "At the conscious level living from the heart reveals our unity as one in the universe."

Oneness? Are you referring to the fact that we are all the same energy?

"You know that the world is one, Michael. When the heart is closed, life's gifts cannot enter it. You cannot live with a locked heart. So to remove the tension that is holding you back in becoming who you are and where you want to be, realize that you just need to open your heart."

I smiled at Tom in the moment. It makes more sense to forget the forgiveness!

"Forget the forgiveness!" Tom replied. "Just commit with your heart and you will find the answers that exist within. It all starts here in the heart, Michael. When you focus on opening the door you are able to close another enabling you to move in the direction you choose for your life."

I guess being able to forget instead of forgive enables you to realize that we are all the same, Tom!

"When you forget you acknowledge that you and the people around you are more than just human. You see them as a pieces of you, Michael."

In essence we are all the same!

"Yes, when you look at people from your heart you will also see yourself in them. When you chastised them for the past you are talking to yourself. And when you hang on to your judgments of their actions you are doing that as it applies to your life."

That is so true, Tom! Most of the time we are only talking to ourselves when addressing others.

"That is what forgiveness ignores, Michael!" Tom explained. Forget about looking for answers from the past and honor the present as it is the only helpful strategy you have to successfully transform the future direction of your life."

Again, Tom disappeared. All I could hear was Tom screaming, "Forget the Forgiveness" as he tackled yet another monster of a wave. In the glory of the morning sunrise I consciously made my first commitment to navigating my life along a different path. Slowly I was surrendering what little resistance I had left. So it made total sense to continue that surrender with being able to forget the forgiveness. Forget the forgiveness is what I repeated the remainder of the morning of the third day in May as I continued to renew my love for the soulful art of surfing and the inner power I had ignored for almost all of my entire life.

Reflection

"No pessimist ever discovered the secrets of the stars or sailed to an
uncharted land or opened a new heaven to the human spirit."
-Helen Keller-

During the time after I proposed to Lisa I remember the planning of our
wedding. Everything in detail from the location, the flowers, catering,
invitations and the actual wedding parties! Lisa was immaculate when it came to
details and would have been quite comfortable engaging herself in the
organization of such a crowning affair all on her own. However, like our life had
been up to that point she wanted to do it as a team. In the best interest of our
powerful love I was with her during the process every step of the way in any
capacity that I could be of service. Lisa wanted the wedding to be perfect. I on
the other hand wanted us to continue being the perfect couple. Something I felt
we had been all along.

When it came down to it the entire process of planning our wedding went
extremely smooth. The location was an easy decision. We chose a park
overlooking Monterey Beach. Lisa's aunt was a floral designer from the mid-
west and was tickled to death when we asked her to help us with the particulars.
The food was catered by the executive chef from her father's country club. A
fashion house in Los Angeles designed the wedding dress. The minister was a
family friend that we had both known since we were children. A jeweler in San
Francisco made our rings. Every last detail was accounted for except for one
thing.

Lisa and I had to choose members for our wedding party. Of course both
sets of parents were going to be in attendance. However, Lisa invited her sister
to be the maid of honor, three close friends and her aunt to accompany her as
bridesmaids. I on the other hand had to match her numbers for my party,
something that would prove to be extremely difficult.

After deliberating at great length we both brainstormed the qualities that
should exemplify a best man. In most cases the person is a brother or a best
friend. Neither of which I had at the time of our wedding. The death of my
brother meant not only the loss of a family member but it represented the end
of my relationship with the nearest and dearest friend I had in the world. My
brother was without a doubt my best friend. The only other friend I had at the
time was Lisa and asking her to be my best man didn't seem appropriate with her
as the bride. Don't get me wrong. We had numerous friends and acquaintances,

however, none of them sincere enough to stand beside me in matrimony.

Lisa and I managed to grind out a list of potential hopefuls to comprise my groomsmen. They consisted of two college pals from my Stanford days and Lisa's younger brother who I barely knew. Asking her bother was a kind gesture in getting to connect with him. As for the college crew, they were only filling a void. However, the best man vacancy remained at-large down to the last days before the gala event.

My heart was heavy at the time of the wedding. I remembered experiencing emotions flowing through my body that I never knew existed. I cried when I heard sincere words. I laughed at the corniest of jokes. I hugged people I at one time in my life would have rather killed and I spoke with love in my voice to everyone. It felt as though I was reaching a state of inner peace whatever that was. However, my full arrangement of assuming inner content was delayed by the outstanding question as to who would I choose as a best man.

The only person that I believed could represent my best interests was my dead brother. I knew it. I felt it and Lisa understood the concern despite the fact that she never had a chance to meet him. You see in spite of the fact that he accidentally shot himself years ago, removing himself from the lives of his family I was still able to converse with him every night in my dreams. As soon as my head hit the pillow my brother and I would enter some deep conversations. We still had a strong bond in the wake of his physical absence. However, resurrecting the dead for our wedding wasn't exactly an option we had the power to make. So Lisa came to me the night before our wedding with what would have seemed like a ridiculous idea to most, but for me it was sensational.

Lisa suggested that since my brother would most likely be in attendance spiritually at the wedding there was no reason he couldn't be my best man. At first, the idea seemed out in left field. However, it was wrapped in sincerity from Lisa's heart. Yet again, Lisa touched me with the gesture. Indeed I was growing closer and closer to her each and everyday. Lisa explained that she had it all figured out. She had a sharp photograph of my brother enlarged and framed ready to accompany us at the alter.

The idea would be to place the picture on a stand beside me. The photo would be set next to the wedding rings for my brother's spirit to protect. Physically and spiritually he would be in our presence on the one day that meant the most. One of the most important events in our lives! Our wedding. Not only that, it meant I had the best man for the job. My brother! However, one last detail was still yet to be accomplished. I still had to ask my brother if being my best man was something he would agree with.

At 7 a.m. the morning of our wedding I drove out to the gravesite where my little brother was laid to rest. Kneeling down, I placed a bouquet of colorful flowers near the tombstone. It was the first time I went to physically visit him since the funeral so many years ago. I told him about college. We talked extensively about Lisa, the girl of my dreams. And of course the upcoming wedding. It was at that very moment when I asked my brother if he would join me as my best man. Crazy enough to say, but I felt a surge of energy in the moments following my invitation to him. I took that sign as a positive reply.

The wedding took place at sunset on the beautiful Monterey Peninsula. I married the love of my life with the people that meant the most to both of us on hand. Most of all, my brother was able to be a major part of such an important day in my life. The day I married Lisa signified a new beginning and the return of my best friend. Once again, I felt him in my heart as he stood with us in spirit the entire day. I knew he was there. He surrounded all of us with his energy. It was comforting to know that he was there for me just as I had tried to be for him. From that point on I came to realize that I left the differences surrounding his death behind for a day. It was definitely a new beginning in life and perhaps for my brother and I.

Chapter Nine:
The Fourth Day in May:
Honoring the Past

"Where I was born and where I have lived is unimportant. It is what
I have done with where I have been that should be of interest.
-Georgia O'Keefe-

That afternoon as I was making my way towards Tom's beach retreat when
an old convertible SUV pulled in behind me. The driver of the vehicle sounded
the horn a few times as I scurried to get out of his way. Looking back to catch
a glimpse of the driver I should have recognized that such a surf-mobile could
only be that of Tom's. He was in the middle of pulling off to the side of the road
to greet me.

What is this? I asked him as we approached each other.

"Get in partner. My office is closed for the day," He said.

I laughed at his remark as I made my way to the passenger side of the SUV.
It was an old classic convertible jeep that had two long-boards protruding from
its rear.

"Ready to witness something truly remarkable, Michael?" Tom asked me.

Sure! Why not? I replied.

Tom hit the accelerator and we were off cruising down the coastline stretch
of highway on the gorgeous Monterey peninsula. It was a warm but overcast
day. Some dense fog had been rolling in off the ocean protecting the sun from

reaching us. It added a definite spiritual setting for our afternoon getaway.

"Michael!" Tom said. "Reflecting back on our meeting the other day we discussed forgetting the past instead of forgiving it."

Yes, I remember that morning quite vividly! So what?

"Well, I know you have been spending a great deal of time looking back on your life up to this point as we have discussed."

Tom, there is no secret that I would love to change what has already taken place if I could.

"I understand that fully," Tom replied.

So what is your point?

"I want to be very clear with you! When I mentioned being able to forget the past instead of forgiving it I meant for you to let go of the resentment you have been carrying."

Right! I understand your point.

"However, I want to clarify how that relates to your past," Tom stated.

Sure! I have no problem with you clarifying that.

Tom pulled his jeep off the highway along seventeen-mile drive. We proceeded to enter a parking area overlooking the ocean. The sign ahead of us revealed the location we were at. It was a popular parkland site in the area. A place I had never been before despite being familiar with the Monterey region. I was a little confused as to why Tom had taken me there. As we exited Tom's SUV we walked for about 10 minutes or so down an old worn out gravel path mixed with sand before coming to an opening in a brush of trees.

Beyond the opening we could see some dense fog some 300 yards out over the ocean. The area we reached was very elevated and the wind was cool. Other than the fog all we could see were the cliff and rock formations that had been carved out over the centuries due to the effects of Mother Nature. It resulted in a series of quaint inlets nestled among a fortress of rocks below. It was a truly amazing showcase for us to see all from a perch atop the cliff side. However, it was not the only spectacle that Tom had brought me to see.

I followed Tom down a winding path that had been created perhaps by thousands of people over the years. It was a pathway to witness a truly glorious portrait. As we reached a corner along the path I could see a well-defined fortress of sediment jutting in a straight passage away from the shoreline. With an ancient appeal esthetically the structure looked like something formed from the architectural period of Rome. The glory of the moment came from a striking, yet dignified 500 year-old cypress tree that statuesquely appeared to be guarding the point like a lone soldier protecting his troops. It was a five hundred year old cypress tree, called the "Lone Cypress". And according to Tom it has stood alone for centuries attached to the rocky formation overlooking the Monterey Coastline.

I couldn't help but wonder if my eyes had deceived me with what I was seeing. It was hard to believe that it was possible for the "Lone Cypress", a tree nonetheless, to stand alone at the mercy of the elements in such an uncharacteristic place to locate. It was amazing that the howling winds and treacherous surf allowed the natural beauty to survive in its domain for all of those centuries.

"What do you think?" Tom shouted.

That is unreal! I stated in disbelief.

"Isn't that a miracle of nature in all its perfection, Michael."

Without a doubt! I responded in amazement of the sight before me.

Tom stared for a moment awestruck at the sight. "That tree is a survivor!"

It has to be if it has been there that long.

"The Lone Cypress represents fortification," Tom explained.

Years ago it must have stood in the presence of others of its kind?

"If the tree could speak it would certainly have a remarkable story. However, in my opinion the image tells it all!"

If it could tell its story I cannot help but wonder if it would express the desire to have the other trees back?

"We will never know, Michael. But we do know one thing is for sure."

And what is that?

"That you believe the flawless piece of perfection in front of you would want to change its past," Tom stated in a serious tone.

Yes, I believe it would.

"To change its past, Michael?"

I think it would want to have others around or at least a change of venue, Tom.

"What is it that makes you so sure of that, Michael?"

I think because I would want to change the situation if I was in that position.

"Just like you want to change your past every waking day of your life?"

Just like my past! I admitted.

"You must see Michael that the universe sees it differently," Tom replied.

How do you mean?

"Michael, the past happens for a reason as I am quite sure you recognize thus far."

You mean the past was meant to occur for a reason?

"Absolutely!" Tom replied. "The past, your past consists of a series of experiences that were meant to happen in order to propel your life to where it is today."

And what a life that turned out to be, I replied sarcastically. A pathetic life I want so very much to change. It is an absolute disaster wouldn't you agree!

"Well, you might as well understand that what has happened in the past and where you are right now cannot change no matter how hard you try!"

I know! It was suppose to play out like this, right?

"Just like the tree, Michael!" Tom replied.

We paused our conversation for a brief time as we admired the natural wonder before us.

"The universe is perfect as you will come to see, Michael!" Tom said.

It doesn't feel so perfect, Tom.

"I have explained the idea of forgetting the resentment you have for your past already, Michael. However, I am not asking you to completely wipe it out."

Now you have me confused.

"The past was meant to happen the way it has. You have to stop challenging it, Michael. It supplied you with some profound experiences from which to learn from during the remainder of your journey called life."

Yes, but look at what I have done with those experiences. I said. I have destroyed my life!

"Michael, I know you feel as though you have destroyed your life but the reality is that you haven't at all."

So what would you call it then?

"Remember, your identity doesn't exist in your money, titles, cars, material, your mistakes and certainly not your past."

Yes! I remember that we are none of these things, I replied.

"Also remember that you are not your actions, words, behaviors or the failures that you perceive yourself to be."

So, the destruction that I believe has occurred has come from the same tainted mind we have been discussing throughout our time together?

"Right, again! By spending all of that time in your head the way you are you are right where your ego wants you to be. That way it is allowed to run free and it is clearly doing that to you as we speak."

I think I see your point!

"The ego loves your past. It loves sifting through the events that have already occurred because it can find a way to relive them. It never lets go of the old information so thereby it uses it to fuel its ever growing sense of self."

So the more time I spend researching the past for answers the greater momentum my ego builds, Tom?

"Yes sir! The two things that fuel the ego the most are your recounts of the past and the desperate yearning for the future."

Again, living in the head supplies my ego with further growth.

"The two most common practices of our minds is relive the past and look forward to the future."

So what is wrong with that?

"If you constantly live in the past how is it possible to change the course of your direction in the present. You cannot alter your future by captaining your ship in the exact same manner as your previous voyage."

So I have obviously lost my way?

"You haven't necessarily lost your way, Michael! I think it is fair to say that you have disconnected from your inner power by allowing your ego to take over."

So if you aren't looking to the past for answers or the future for change what else is there to do?

"Well, that is why things appear so bleak to you, Michael!" Tom said. "Because you see no other avenues for escape. So you rely on what feels most natural to you."

So what can I do, Tom.

"You need to reconnect with your inner self as we have discussed previously," Tom replied.

And how can I do that?

Tom pointed to his heart. "Well, that you already have the answer for."

I know! Spend more time in my heart looking for the answers that I have within? Right!

"You got it, Michael! Get out of your head as often as you can because when it tells you enough lies you are bound to start believing them. And it is very clear that you are guilty of that."

I appeared rattled by the topic we were engaged in. That's it?

"There are two more strategies you must become familiar with to accomplish the task, Michael."

Oh! And what would those involve?

"First off, I want you to forget the past but remember that there is no contradiction in honoring your past and building a future," Tom explained.

Well, it sounds like you are contradicting what you said about the past and the future just a moment ago, Tom.

"Listen, Michael! You have spent god only knows how long, internally wallowing in your past."

Of course! Yes, thinking "What If" it was different in some way, shape or form.

"And in doing so you are living in your head, hanging on to the resentment towards your past in the meantime."

I cannot help but blame my past for where I am today. I have only myself to blame for that! I admitted.

Tom shouted. "Why must you continually torture yourself for something that will never change unless you allow it too?"

So I should forget it in your opinion?

"For starters, forget about living in your head! What does the negativity move you closer to accomplishing in your present life, Michael."

I can't honestly say, Tom.

"So why not forget the resentment? Forget living in your mind! Forget the overpowering ego! And embrace everything you have gone through with acceptance," Tom shouted.

The past is all that seems familiar to me right now, Tom.

"And that is precisely why people like you, Michael, choose to live and hold on to the past. Simply because it is all you know how to do! It is exactly what you are doing, Michael."

You mean I am searching for answers in a place that they don't exist?

"Constantly replaying the past only places you in the same positions, states and thoughts that are attached to a small piece of your history, Michael."

I will openly admit that, Tom.

"If your living in a world that you cannot alter, how do you expect to power your life in the present?"

I am not sure what you are getting at?

"It's the second task you have to put in place, Michael!" Tom replied.

Well, don't keep me in suspense.

"Drudging up the past is something you understand to be a comfortable place to live from. In addition, many people like yourself also choose to focus towards the future in order to escape the past."

Obviously, I am hoping for a better tomorrow, Tom.

"However, you are missing something important in between, Michael!"

Really! What could that be?

"You tell me! What lies between the past and the future, Michael?"

The present, I suppose, I answered.

Tom shouted in excitement. "Right! The now. The present. Whatever you want to call it, Michael!"

So what about it?

"It is your mind that has instilled a fear inside you that keeps you either in the past or focused on the future. It's a safe place to be because it is a known entity for you. The problem however, is that by devoting your trust to these arenas in search of the perceived answers you facilitate an attachment that's purpose only serves to disconnect you from the navigation of your life in the present."

I see your point, Tom!

"So if you have surrendered your present life for refuge in the past or for the expectations of the future two questions remain outstanding."

And those would be?

"First, who is navigating your life right now? And secondly, do you think you can follow the same path you always have and discover a different outcome?" Tom replied.

I suppose no one is captaining my ship at present! I said in disbelief.

"Maybe not! However, I am more inclined to direct you to the fact that your unconscious self is running your life course but just not in the direction I think you would prefer."

I also believe that you cannot solve a problem with the same mindset that created it, Tom.

"Good, Michael! So now you have answered the second question. So what else do you have left?"

The present!

"And where does the present lie?"

In your heart! I replied with great confidence.

"Not so fast, Michael! The present is a state of consciousness that you will soon begin to not only understand but also put to practice. However, it's origin lies in the powerful connection between your head and your heart. The connection that is established between the physical and spiritual worlds! A connection that is commanded by your inner power! Based on the person you want the world to see revealed."

So I have been lacking the vision to proactively guide my life journey?

"You were simply disconnected allowing the mind to run the show, Michael!" Tom replied. "So, remember to honor what your past has presented to you. Learn the lessons that it provided you using the knowledge you have today, in the present. When you finally put an end to recounting the steps of your past you will flourish from the direction in which your heart will lead you."

You want me to honor the past but forget the resentment?

"I am asking you to consider seeing the world from a different vantage point, Michael. Quite simply a much better place! By taking the knowledge from your past that has already been stored, look to the heart for the answers. In doing so you automatically pay honor to the events that have historically taken place without ignoring them. In that capacity your inner power will assume the responsibility of recalibrating you in the present. Hence, the motion of plotting your course for the future! However, remember that the power comprising you is at its height when you exist in a state of present time consciousness."

I can understand fully what you are getting at! I finally see the link between the two, I admitted.

"The really cool thing about the perfection of the universe and you is that everyday is a new day, Michael!" Tom shouted in joy.

I could use a few new days.

"Michael, understand that you are not your past. So come out from behind it. Stop hiding in the conflicting comfort that it provides you. If you keep on living in the past the hole in your heart that is so clearly evident is only going to get larger and larger with every trip down memory lane."

I guess I need to reconnect and redirect, Tom, I suppose.

"You must reconnect with the power within to seal the wound in your heart allowing yourself the opportunity to make it your driving force."

It all makes complete sense, I admitted.

Each and every moment I spent with Tom the answers that lie beneath seemed to surface. Tom remarked that he had a call he had to make on his cell phone. Apologizing for interrupting our progress it appeared to be a case of urgency that required his time for the moment. We agreed to meet at his jeep in the next ten to fifteen minutes to head back to the center. That left me the opportunity to plant myself on a patch of nearby grass overlooking the wonder, stillness and posterity of "The Lone Cypress".

Gazing at its perfection mounted in fortitude atop its rocky home I remember pondering the idea of whether it was meant to be. It was in that moment that I consciously understood what it was that seemed to be keeping me from capturing my inner spirit. Me! I didn't actually see it until Tom and I had paused our discussion that day. Many times before I would have blazed such an attack with my clouded ego. However, today I embraced my heart by vowing to point my life in whatever direction it revealed. The only way to embrace the newest chapter on my journey would be to reconnect with the present that I was missing out on. To be successful I would have to start living with the truth of the heart instead of the lies of my mind. And it is the heart that holds the truth. As I watched the fog surround the "Lone Cypress" I came to a knowing that I was destined to capture the life I was wanting in the moment. In the present! Finally at last! I was on the right track for once in my life.

Reflection

"The friend who understands you creates you."
-Romain Rolland-

Six months after Lisa and I were married friends of her parents loaned us their mountain retreat overlooking the Rockies in Aspen, Colorado. When we arrived the snowfall in the mountains was plentiful as we intended to do some pretty heavy skiing during our time there. Late one afternoon amidst a winter blizzard Lisa and I took a break from the slopes to uncork a bottle of red wine in front of a roaring fire. Toasting our marriage the topic quickly turned to children.

Lisa without a doubt had motherly aspirations. After all, it made complete sense to me as she came from a large family herself. Furthermore, even before we were married the women from her side of the family fostered the notion of pregnancy. Not only that I could see the look in Lisa's eyes when we came across a baby or toddler in public. She had a nurturing way about her, a natural so to speak. I knew those fragments of human spirit came to life over the idea of us having a family.

As for myself! I grew up in a military household. We were anything but nurtured as children. That is not to say that my parents didn't love us! However, we were taught to be both mentally and physically tough. Displaying signs of emotion in our family was interpreted as a weakness. My parents weren't the affectionate types with each other so it wasn't hard to understand why as children my brother and I were never hugged or kissed. The words "I love you" were not used with any regularity either. Affection in our household was an occasional pat on the back or verbal commendation for a task well done.

So for me the idea of beginning a family of my own was quite terrifying. Primarily because I had such overpowering aspirations for my professional life! My career took precedents over everything but Lisa at that time. I knew that my work would demand long laborious hours to escalate to the heights I aspired to reach. And that is why the idea of children was not at the top of my list of things that needed to be done.

My personal feelings at the time revolved around bringing a child into the world to appease the hopes of generations before us only to grow-up one parent shy of the two it deserved. And that one absentee parent could admittedly be me. At least until I ascended the corporate ladder that I intended to climb! After that there is no telling whether or not I would be ready to consider assuming the important role of becoming a parent. The bottom line was that I was jaded by my own selfishness at the time to consider the possibilities of what it would mean to be selfless. My theory applied not only to our discussion on children but also towards aspects of life in general.

As we sat beside a roaring fire the snow spiraled continuously outside the window. Lisa and I continued our discussion on parenthood. Lisa understood exactly where I was coming from. I knew her and she knew me. I never once kept my feelings regarding the issue of family bottled up inside. I always had the audacity to tell her precisely my thoughts surrounding the topic. For that I believe Lisa appreciated my honesty because it was something she openly admitted. It was not as though I didn't want children in our life. However, I believed morally the timing couldn't be worse.

If starting a family was something that I was going to participate in I was bound and determined that I was going to do it the right way. If that meant having a child later in life than so be it. Leaving Lisa alone with the responsibility of raising a child meant a certain level of neglect on my behalf. And that however, wasn't going to happen as long as I had a say in the matter. No way would that fall back on my head if things didn't turn out.

Even before our wedding Lisa and I would playfully entertain the idea of children's names as we sunned ourselves on the beach. What the product of our love would look like and how they would express themselves, as they grew older was something that every couple engaged in it seemed. However, for me it wasn't always so much a game. I often became frustrated with the flirting around we did on the topic. I questioned what I had to possibly offer as a father. I deliberated often, regarding the priority of family or my career.

The corporate world executives had a certain status within their respective companies to uphold. Upon reaching that pinnacle many sacrifices would have to continuously be made. And that included any form of home life. It was usually the nannies, housekeepers and day care centers that spent most of the time raising the children. An all too real occurrence that Lisa and I witnessed firsthand. Something that didn't seem like a healthy decision as far as I was concerned!

Lisa and I both agreed that we were in no rush to start a family. With my career soaring through the ranks and hers taking on new evolution we both reconciled that children just didn't fit at the moment. However, like most couples we talked about family before any surprises popped up. Establishing a list of importance is something that we both achieved that afternoon. It included waiting for the time being to assess our lives down the road to avoid raising kids in an empty home. We both agreed that our careers were the focus at the moment.

I experienced firsthand what it meant to grow up in a broken family. My mother was left with the difficult task of raising two young boys on her own as my father was absent much of the time due to military obligations. I cannot begin to describe the stress involved with such a job. The restless nights, the constant running around, the organization, the emotions and the responsibility that came with raising kids! My interpretation of the experience hardly brings meaning to the sacrifices my mother made for us.

I was close with my mother. There were numerous times where I witnessed her crying herself to sleep at night while my father was away. I am sure the pressures of being a good parent alone became enough to overwhelm her let alone the idea of giving up much of her own life for us. I mean lets face it! She was the mother, father, cook, maid, cleaner, driver, gardener, shopper, bookkeeper and a whole lot more all rolled into one title. It wasn't hard to see that my father had it easy. In my opinion I think he enjoyed his time away. He never tried to make up for it with my mother or us kids when he was around.

I can honestly admit that over the years my mother never once complained about her life openly. She sacrificed everything for my brother and I. We were all she had in the world. There was no social circle. No vacations. No days at the spa. No time alone except that in which we were in school and even then I am sure she had a million other jobs to do.

There wasn't a doubt in my mind that she resented my father for leaving her in the position she was in. With the toughest of tasks raising two young children practically on her own! I believe she grew to accept her role over the years. Based on her character, walking out on us wasn't an option. However, her acceptance placed an emotional strain on her relationship with my father. With Dad being away most of the time on secret missions you would never hear the two on the phone or in person engage in any meaningful conversation long enough to know.

But the dark circles and the signs of exhaustion on my mothers face told the real story. In fact, my brother and I watched her age rapidly before our eyes. Looking some twenty years older than her actual middle age. There was no doubt that the sacrifices she made with the position she was placed in contributed to her aging equation. Knowing that it was her path in life I am sure didn't ease the burden either.

As for my brother and I we had it easy. We tried to help out as much as we could. It was hard not to be sympathetic to my mother's situation. It wasn't a tough life. Its not like we were poor, starving kids. But after all we were just kids. So we spent most of our time just being kids as my mother slaved away to provide for us. There really wasn't anything we didn't have. Dad made great money that afforded us a middle class lifestyle. The only thing we didn't have was the typical mother and father relationship that other children around us experienced.

My mother may have seen it differently but we understood even as kids what she was going through. And that is why as an adult my views on the subject of family remained so strong. My experience growing up in the fashion I was subjected to I vowed that I would never do to Lisa what my father had done to my mother. A promise that I openly made to Lisa that day as we watched the snow fall in the beautiful Rocky Mountains.

Chapter Ten:
The Fifth Day in May:
Cleansing Our Fears

"Our doubt's are traitors, And make us lose the good
we oft might win, By fearing to attempt."
-William Shakespeare-

The morning of the fifth day in May I awoke stumbling toward the restroom only to notice a slip of paper that had been placed underneath my door. It was a note from Tom in regards to our forthcoming afternoon meeting. The note had indicated that I was supposed to meet the center's driver in the lobby that afternoon, as he would be taking me to a different site to meet with Tom.

I remember thinking how mysterious it all was. Nonetheless, I was extremely excited about what was to come in the hours ahead. It wasn't just the excitement surrounding the next lesson either. Indeed that intrigued me however the change in location also meant that Tom had something up his sleeve. As I had come to learn Tom was never one to spend a dull day talking about meaningless information.

After joining the center's driver we journeyed down the coast for about 45 minutes until we arrived at a national park. As soon as I exited the van Tom greeted me wearing hiking apparel.

No surfboards by the looks of it today, I said to Tom as we shook hands.

"Not today, Michael!" Tom smiled. "But that doesn't mean that I haven't got something wild and crazy for you to do."

Whatever it is I am sure it will be adventurous!

I followed Tom as we walked down a color marked trail mapped in the park. It was one of several we had to choose from but Tom seemed to know exactly where we were going. As we descended upon the altering terrain of flats and hills we engaged in what I believed was the next topic on the agenda.

"So how are you doing inside that body of yours, Michael?" Tom asked.

I would say pretty well! I guess!

"Michael, I noticed that your incredibly up for our meetings but I can't help but wonder if you are still spending too much time in your head after. That ritual will only slow your increasing momentum."

I have to admit that I have been subjecting myself to the flip-flop approach. After our talks of late you have ignited me with the desire to take on the world. And then somehow my ego enters the picture and drops me down a few notches.

"How about the urge to disappear into the world of drugs, Michael?"

Surprisingly, between the meetings, your coaching and my new-found mental outlook I have managed to focus on my personal development instead of the chemical side of things. I am starting to understand what you meant when you talked about the natural highs in life.

"That's awesome, Michael! Glad to hear it! Today I promise you will experience another one of those highs."

In fact, I have succumbed to a different type of internal conflict.

"Oh! What does that entail? Tom said curiously.

It feels like a crossroads between internally punishing myself for my past actions and rebuilding a new life that eats at me.

"Well, I take it back! Your life is almost on the right track, Michael."

Most days I just feel defeated and I can't quite shake the pull it has on me.

"Funny you mention that, Michael! When defeat overtakes a man, the most logical and easiest thing to do is quit. That is exactly what the majority of people do. They quit! They give up!" Tom shouted.

I shook my head in agreement. I can understand why!

"The question is will that be you, Mr. Jamieson? Do you have it in you to continue on the path that has been presented before you?"

There is no way I will quit that easily. It's just that I have been feeling the pressure of late internally and it still manages to periodically disrupt my life.

"No one said it was going to be easy, Michael. Let me remind you of one more thing!" What's that?

"Remember to enjoy the process along the way. Both the good and the bad!

Enjoy the lessons you will learn and apply them to your life."

I must admit that back at the "Lone Cypress" the other day I made a commitment to my own personal transformation.

"Now that is great!" Tom yelled.

However, fifty percent of me feel's as though I have the power to control my own thoughts and the other half is working against me. The conflict is pulling me in different directions and I am unsure about how to gain control.

"Michael, that will all change in due time to a much larger percentage. In the mean time enjoy the process and stop being so eager to go from point A to point B overnight. As we study the art of turning defeat into the stepping stones of opportunity you will understand what I am referring too," Tom stated with a huge grin on his face.

As we came to a bend in the path I could see a brick stone terrace situated about fifty feet ahead of us. As we approached the natural balcony constructed from the past it offered us a rather stunning view of yet another wondrous creation of nature. Tom and I stood peering into a deep valley that revealed a towering waterfall as its backdrop. The waterfall itself must have been hundreds of feet in height as it poured a steady stream of water and mist onto a collection of rocks below a thundering gorge.

"Fabulous!" Tom shouted into the valley only to hear his echo continue on.

However, it wasn't long until we both heard that echo return. Instead, the echo of fabulous was from another source that came from a different direction. Where did it come from I wondered? However, my perplexity vanished in my overwhelming appreciation for the scenery bestowed upon us.

"Looks pretty awesome from up here wouldn't you say, Michael?

Absolutely! I replied.

"Come on, Michael! There is a lot more in store. Let's get a closer look."

So we continued our trek down the winding path with a more moderate pace than that of before. The light of the day was blocked by the dense foliage that came from the forest canopy as our journey continued! It was gradually getting darker the deeper we went along the path.

"I can understand, Michael, your insatiable desire to change your life."

What else can I do, Tom?

"Well, that's just it! You are so focused on how you are going to change your life that you have forgotten to answer why you want to change it," Tom shouted in frustration.

Oh! Trust me I know exactly why I want to change my life.

"Is that so?"

Yes. As a matter of fact I want my job, my wife and my child all back in my life.

Tom broke out laughing.

"Is that Michael I am hearing or that pesky former self of yours again?"

I am glad you find it amusing! I stated in frustration.

"Yes! It's confirmed. The ego is at work!"

What are you trying to do?

Tom apologized. "You approach your life as if it were in great need of a boost just like a drug addict needs a fix."

Continue! I said intrigued by the sudden change in the conversation.

"Only what you are not giving is lacking in a situation, Michael."

I missed that, Tom.

"You need to bring more to the table, my friend."

How so?

"Remember our previous discussions centering around what you are and what you are here on earth to do? Have you taken a look inside for the answers that have been holding you back?"

I assume that I still have yet to let go, I admitted to Tom.

"What are you waiting for, Michael? Why do you think we have been spending so much time opening your eyes to the inner power that compromises you?"

So I know where to look for the answers.

Tom's voice began to rise sharply. "No! Michael. These are the foundations that will allow you to see who it is you actually are deep inside that resilient body that you are renting."

Right! I remember.

"To foster the conclusion as to why you should change your life direction by allowing you to see that you are in actual command of the journey."

Yes, I just want to know how to do that! I pleaded to Tom in desperation.

"A big enough why, will always figure out how, Michael!"

I peered down at the forest floor. Please stop talking in riddles, Tom!

"Michael, you already understand that the true answers to guide your life lie inside your heart. I cannot force you to look there or listen to what it tells you. However, I have unveiled to you the breeding ground that initiates personal transformation."

I know you cannot make me change, I admitted openly.

"Well than why are you continuously pleading with me to reactively show you the way when all you need to do is proactively bring more to the table."

I guess I just feel lost!

We paused our walk as Tom pointed to my chest. "No one else is going to shift your life direction unless you consciously want it bad enough to step up to the table. Go back to last week, Michael. Remember when we discussed how goals in today's world are a popular stigma."

I thought that we determined that goals were the illusion of the physical world, Tom?

"Yes, they can be if you sacrifice your principles, integrity and values to achieve what someone else has convinced your ego it needs to acquire."

Okay! I replied. I follow you.

"Ask yourself, once again, if this truly resonates from the real Michael! Compromising your own desires to get what someone else wants for you?"

I understand your point, Tom.

"Well, if you understand the key principle than why are you still using the very same methods you always have to reconstruct your life?"

My eyes began to well up with tears. Because it is all I know how to do, Tom!

Tom managed a sincere smile. "We have already shot that defense full of holes, Michael, but nice try nonetheless. Getting emanates from your true being. The power that you have learned about, but haven't yet become."

The being inside me that is trying to get out!

"Yes! Getting what you really want stems from your soul, it mirrors your true self and it becomes your conscious state of mind."

So it comes from my understanding why? I asked Tom.

"When the why becomes big enough, the how is revealed. Stop asking how because I believe you already know the answers. You see it comes from the heart without the cloak of fear that has been holding you back, Michael."

You mean questions like why I want to change my life? Why I want my family back?

"Yes, Michael! Ask your heart those very same questions and stop fearing the answers that it will begin to reveal."

You think I fear the answers?

"It couldn't be any more apparent that you fear the answers that you already know you have or you wouldn't be resisting the process of moving on. All you need to do is embrace the flurry of fear that exists in your mind for what it is. It clearly overshadows the answers that lie in your heart."

Is that where the why is, Tom?

Tom took a sincere tone of voice.

"That is something you will have to find out on your own, Michael."

As we proceeded around a bend in the trail we began walking quite vigorously towards a clearing leading up to the waterfall. As we continued our approach to the apex of the spectacle we were met by five men all wearing similar attire to Tom's. Furthermore, they adorned helmets, climbing gear and heavy-duty gloves. The entire perimeter surrounding the waterfall was scattered with rock climbing paraphernalia. In that instant I knew the echo we heard in return to Tom's earlier had been from someone in the group. My heart started racing. The fear of the unknown that minute consumed me. I was terrified of heights and I sensed that the next suggestion coming from Tom had much more to do with climbing than it had to do with coaching.

It was revealed that the group we met at the waterfall was Tom's rock climbing club. They met regularly to climb and repel structures such as the waterfall we had previously admired. And that pretty much summed up my destiny for that afternoon. The description of Tom that had existed in my mind went from off the wall shrink to one bordering on insanity. I was in a bind and I knew it. I would have to do something outside of my comfort zone to learn some type of predetermined lesson. However, I wasn't sure of the nature of the task just yet. That is what worried me the most.

"I sense you know what we are about to participate in today!" Tom stated with a mischievous smirk on his face.

Kind of! My intuition tells me that it is also one of my greatest fears.

"Obviously you have never done the kind of activity we are about to engage in before, Michael?"

Are you kidding me? I am deathly afraid of heights Tom!

"I thought you believed you had the power to control your thoughts to some degree?"

Yeah! Well apparently that theory didn't hold up. What's even worse is that I am more worried about your crazy self in relation to my executing the task safely.

Tom laughed in excitement and I could do nothing else but join him with the nervousness I felt in the moment. The group of climbers outfitted me with the proper ensemble of gear to repel the waterfall with Tom. Like the idea or not I was going down the proverbial mountain in order to learn a lesson that Tom was about to instill within me. Following a brief tutorial addressing the finer points of rock climbing Tom and I together were about to embark on one of my greatest fears.

"Michael!" Tom shouted.

Yes! I replied.

"Are you scared yet?"

I am 1000% terrified you crazy shrink!

"Are you ready?"

Ask me in about an hour! I stated sarcastically.

"For too long you have been studying the art of failure. In my opinion that is your greatest fear. You fear the world of unknowns because you believe you don't have the knowledge that exists in it to lead to your success."

Isn't that called reality?

Tom yelled again. "I call it the weakness of mankind."

How so?

"It represents the human races familiarity with the word 'Impossible'. A fear consciousness that has poisoned their minds! One that I hope to help you alter in the next several minutes," Tom shouted with great vigor.

And off we went! In that second we were floating in the air dangling high above the soaring peak of the waterfall. Moving through its mist I could feel my feet heavy below me. I urged myself to avoid the thought of looking down. My greatest fear was being lived out as I hung paralyzed from a rope high above the treacherous valley beneath me. For a moment I lost sight of my fear as I considered Tom's words regarding me. I am not sure if it was his intention but Tom had sparked my curiosity to learn more on the subject that obviously played a major role in my development as a spiritual being in the physical experience.

The shouting coming from Tom's direction interrupted my focus. "Michael, do yourself a favor and look down!"

I don't think that is such a good idea, I replied.

"Trust the universe and look down for heavens sake will you!" He screamed.

So I took his advice! I looked down against every last bit of internal resistance I had remaining in my hanging body. I expected a rush of horror but instead I witnessed one awesome vantage point to absorb the breathtaking scenery that nature had provided for us. As I hovered in the air I saw the white water spouting onto a pile of rocks in the gorge below.

Tom was applauding my efforts. "Great job, Michael! Its gets even better!"

And it did! Next, we were lowered underneath the waterfall where I could see a distinct ledge carved in the rock wall beneath the running water. As we descended towards the balcony Tom moved continuously towards me urging me to use my legs to propel forward to reach the rock shelf. Upon reaching the natural perch we were able to pause sitting behind the endless flow of water gushing out into the open air. The sight was truly unbelievable. What was even more captivating for me was the fact that not a drop of fear oozed from my veins the entire time I sat in wonder. A sense of calm had suddenly come over me.

Tom turned towards me. "Let me ask you, Michael! Do you shower every morning before you head off to work?"

I am supposed to answer that ridiculous question, Tom?

"Well do you?" He spat back at me.

As a matter of fact I certainly do! I said. Who doesn't?

"Why do you shower?"

To clean myself from the dirt that accumulates on my body!

"Good hygiene, right! So if you are cleansing your body to leave it fresh for the upcoming day why don't you do the very same chore with your thoughts, Michael?"

I was confused by the shift in questioning. What are you talking about?

"You ever go to bed with the same thoughts on your mind and wake up the next day with the very same mindset?"

For sure I have! All the time!

"Why not cleanse your thoughts as well as your body, Michael? Why not dispose of yesterdays junk before you take it into spoiling a new day?"

I am starting to see your analogy! I admitted to Tom.

"You want to captain your own ship in life, Michael, don't you?"

A question you already have the answer for!

"You see the circumstances of your life won't shift until you do!"

Well why is that? I asked intent to hear his response.

"We live in a fear based society! It is anything but love based. Miracles cannot occur consciously when they are plagued by a fear based mind."

What kind of miracles are you referring to, Tom?

"Everyday miracles that happen in your life when your inner spirit, your real self is revealed."

I am a little confused with regards to cleansing and these miracles you are talking about.

"You must cleanse the negativity of your thoughts to create a fresh course for your own experience in life. If not it clouds the open road ahead."

I understand your point!

"Why let your past and future fears drive your life in the present, Michael?"

I think most people just unconsciously follow along.

"Yes they do, Michael! But why do you think they fail to question it?"

I am not quite sure!

"Here is how it all works!" Tom exclaimed. "Your ego counters your real self!"

149

I already recognize that concept.

"So you understand that your mind takes control of your life and clouds your heart!"

Right! I remember.

"Your ego makes you believe, through past experiences, what I call the 'known'. It also has an intense fear of the ego created 'unknown's'. In fact, it convinces you in believing that you are unlucky or unfortunate in your life. Most of the time the incredible power overrides the actual consciousness that exists in your heart. A force that serves to position your direction in the present and towards the future."

Your narrating my horrible story again, Tom!

"It happens because we become content with embracing the fear that we see, hear and experience in our lives. Sources like our family, friends and media ingrain them within us. By witnessing these accounts we form beliefs similar to them."

Our beliefs?

"Remember you inherit these beliefs over the course of your life from family, teachers, parents and friends. You believe they come to life when you watch them on television, read them in the newspaper and live them in reality."

They are definitely reinforced in our lives!

"Beliefs cover a wide range of subjects. Things like family, poverty, success, race, politics and life in general. These beliefs become the foundation for your minds perceived views of success in the world."

Interesting point!

"The greatest fear in embarking on the journey of life is that of not being accepted. The fear of not attaining the perceived expectations set forth by those we are closest too. And that fosters an intense fear inside our minds, Michael."

We strive not to disappoint the people we feel are important!

"Yes, but instead you only disappoint yourself unconsciously because you have abandoned your true desires in the process to make others happy."

So that becomes the fear that we are running from?

"No, it is the fear you are running from, Michael!"

How so?

"Transforming yourself into something you are not because you fear the unknown world of not being able to do so is perceived as a failure to the mind. An avoid at all costs measure it has to block the expression of what your heart has to say."

The process of selling out!

"Essentially, you forfeit the connection you had with your soul. Leaving you afraid to express what it actually intends to communicate to not only you but the physical world."

And that is why we are afraid to just be ourselves, Tom?

"You've got it, Michael! That is the grandest fear known to man."

The fear of being your real self! I stated in amazement.

"Yes, because so much time is spent layering thought after thought, belief upon belief in our minds that the result becomes the fear that we might not be accepted if we decide to do things on our own terms."

You mean listening to your own heart?

"These people are called rebels or outcasts because they separate from the herd mentality that exists. You know Michael! The heart is the place of mankind's greatest fear."

And that is why the flurry of negativity becomes a proverbial blizzard over time creating a disconnection within us?

"Yes sir! Fear prevents us from experiencing meaningful growth in our lives. That is why people feel trapped. Unfulfilled in their roles."

I see! I admitted.

"Instead of just holding you back, fear becomes you," Tom stated in a serious voice.

With making his last statement Tom ventured off the rock shelf to continue our descent through the waterfall. I paused to contemplate my fears before motioning to join him. Fifty feet or so below me I could see Tom emerge from behind the waterfall's mist. Together we hung beside the turbulent wonder in mid-air listening to its thunderous sound.

"Most of us fear the unknowns, Michael!"

I suppose it appears easiest to masquerade as something you are not to make it all work, I replied.

"The masking you refer too becomes some peoples consciousness. Something they do and don't even realize it."

I know because I have been doing it for years! I admitted shamefully.

"That's because revealing yourself to the world is risky! It's a very scary thing to become vulnerable. And that is what we fear the most."

In my world you are seen as weak and the hungry wolves feed off of that.

"You can certainly transform your life with a big enough why, Michael. When you do the fear of revealing your real identity becomes easier."

You mean I can overcome the identity I have accepted in my career, my titles and my ego?

"Yes, you can overcome the identity that is encased with fear because these things will all change over time."

I understand, Tom!

"In doing so they have created many unanswered questions regarding your role in life, it's meaning!"

You can say that again! I replied.

"Don't get so attached to the outcome that you don't enjoy the process of transformation, Michael! Self discovery can be an enlightening event."

I find it all so energy draining, I admitted.

"Remove the self defeat by recognizing that a whole world of endless possibilities exists in a place that has all the answers you are in search of. You already know where the answers lie! You just have to get over the fear that you have to begin the search."

So I assume you are referring to the place that I fear the most, Tom?

"You already know, Michael!" Tom replied.

Yes, I believe I do! I admitted again.

"Look at you, Michael! You have already conquered one of your greatest perceived fears today."

What's that?

"Well, your dangling hundreds of feet in the air attached to nothing but a piece of rope aren't you?"

You are absolutely right!

"So how does that feel inside to know that all of your fears are nothing more than a creation of the mind? To break through the things that you believe are holding you back?"

It feels invigorating! I am experiencing what you would call a natural high I suppose!

"Your mind fears the powerful answers that lie in your heart. The mind also is where you are most comfortable in spending the majority of your time for now."

And is that what is preventing me from the transformation I am trying to make?

"Yes! It has had a very powerful hold on you," Tom shouted.

"When your why becomes big enough you will open your heart instead of your mind to the unknown place you previously feared. And in it you will pick the answers as if they were ripe fruit ready to be eaten. Until your 'why' becomes conscious you will continue to admonish the fear that has been masking your true spirit from its rightful place in the physical world."

So no one will get to see the real Michael?

"Not as long as you are holding him back!" Tom replied.

I guess I need to stop asking you 'how' questions all the time!

"You already know how, Michael! Now all you need to figure out is 'why'! Just remember, that the place you fear the most is also the same place where your potential growth lies," Tom stated with a warm comforting smile.

I just have to get there!

"You will, Michael! But I would rather see you enter your heart for all the right reasons."

What do you mean? I asked him.

"Michael, if you fear the loss of your career, your family, your wife or whatever. You are once again in search of possessions that the ego seeks. I want you to understand that all you have to offer the world is the real you. The spirit that expresses itself from your heart! And when you unveil that remarkable power to the world you will be amazed at the riches that will enter your life."

That all sounds pretty awesome, Tom!

"Yes and you will experience its power very soon my friend! However, please remember one thing for me, Michael!"

Sure!

"Remember that the grandest illusion of humankind is the fear of the unknown!" Tom yelled in excitement.

"So what does that message tell you?"

To just be myself! I stated smiling as if I had just passed one of the toughest tests I had ever taken.

"Put your fears aside and just be yourself," Tom yelled again.

The moment was triumphant for me. Here I was peering down at the world below as we descended alongside the waterfall finally reaching the base of the gorge hundreds of feet beneath us. Standing on some pebbles creating a path underneath the thundering crash of water we collected the rope from above.

A new sense of excitement had overwhelmed my previously energy depleted body. I indeed looked up to the heavens knowing that I had conquered one of my greatest fears that day. I couldn't help but wonder if living from the heart was something I was capable of. And if it was would it feel like I was feeling right now? I relished the idea of making everyday of my life feel like I had won a major victory. With the elation running wild inside me I looked forward to placing a great many fears behind me in the days and weeks to come. Finally, I experienced the natural high that a conscious life had to offer. Something that Tom had frequently talked about. A real high greater than any I had ever been witness to before.

Reflection

"Try not to become a man of success
but rather try to become a man of value."
-Albert Einstein-

At my daughters baptism a poem was read by Lisa's best friend with the purpose of reminding us about life as a child. The poem was one that I would never forget. It was called "A Childs Laughter". It was the first time I had heard it but not the last time I would read it. I had grown to cherish its words and the mental images it provided me in the time that I was away from my daughter, Eva.

A Childs' Laughter

All the bells of heaven may ring,
All the birds in heaven my sing,
All the wells on earth may spring,
All the winds on earth may bring,
All sweet sounds together;
Sweeter for than all the things heard,
Hand of harper, tone of bird,
Sound of woods at sundown stirred,
Welling waters winsome word,
Wind in warm wan weather,

One thing yet there is, that none,
Hearing ere its chime be done,
Know not well the sweetest one,
Heard of man beneath the sun,
Hoped in heaven hereafter;
Soft and strong and loud and light—
Very sound of very light
Heard from mornings' rosiest height—
When the soul of all delight
Fills a child's clear laughter.

Golden bells of welcome rolled
Never faith such notes, nor told
Hours so blithe in tones so bold,
As the radiant mouth of gold
Here that rings forth heaven.
If the golden-crested wren
Were a nightingale—why, then,

Something seen and heard of men
Might be half as sweet as when
Laughs a child of seven.

Algernon Charles Swinburne

It was just a poem for some! However, for me the meaning it had became a part of my life that I never forgot. I found it one afternoon in my office rolled up tight in a scroll with a huge ribbon snuggly placed around its borders. Over a day ending glass of scotch I lamented the poem written in my daughters honor.

Nothing could substitute for the laugh of Eva. It simply brought me to tears seeing the smile on her beautiful face. A smile that lit up even the darkest of my days! Her laugh was so infectious it would always draw me to laughter. Most of all it felt good inside to know that nothing could oppose my daughter's youth. The innocence, the laughter and the happiness she displayed were indeed my comfort during the most trying of times.

It had been a long while since I had seen or heard her laughter but that didn't shun the memories that I had from the past. It was even longer since I had heard the stories of her day that kept her smiling. Not having my daughter in my life made me realize that I had not blissfully laughed myself. Since I made the decision to leave my family behind my life was stripped of any such happiness. Sure I laughed and smiled, but it was never real. It was just imitation. I missed my daughter, but most of all I missed sharing in the hysterical chorus' of laughter that we would always engage in together. Over anything at all we would break out giggling. It was these moments with her that I would always remember because I felt so far removed from the self-imposed pressures of my life. She made me feel safe and innocent just like a child again.

Chapter Eleven:
The Sixth Day in May:
Discovering Your Passion

"The people that get on in this world are the people that get up and look for circumstances that they want and if they don't find them, they make them."
-George Bernard Shaw-

"Michael!" A soft voice spoke in a whisper. "Michael! Wake up," It said.

It was Tom over the intercom waking me for some reason. I thought it was my brother at first as I was engaged in a dream involving him moments before I was interrupted by Tom. It was pitch black outside and the clock displayed 4:30 a.m.

In a raspy voice I responded. I am assuming you need a surf partner and no one else took you up on your offer.

"No, you were the first person I thought of asking," Tom replied.

I will meet you on the beach in say, fifteen minutes or so, Tom!

"Hurry, dude you don't want to miss the sunrise."

See you in a little while.

Half asleep, startled at the reality of having a dream about a real life conversation with my dead brother I rose out of bed in search of my wetsuit. I cracked open the screen door in my room stunned to hear the crash of the surf. It had to be immense to be producing that kind of boom. The wind was gusting quite vigorously. That combination meant for exciting surfing. Why else would

Tom have woken me to join him? My renewed excitement for surfing began to grow since enrolling at the center. Tom was right about one thing. There was something soulful about being one with the universe. Riding a wave created by the same energy comprised of you was a truly remarkable experience when I reflected on it.

I arrived at the beach that morning in the light hue of the moonlight. It was full and part of me stirred in a giggle as that related to the sometimes crazy antics of Tom.

"What are you laughing at?" Tom asked me as I arrived.

You! I said continuing my laugh.

"Why?" Tom replied.

I just noticed that there is a full moon out! So I couldn't help but think what that tends to do to some people, Tom.

"That's right, Michael! Freaks come out at night!"

I guess we are both a little freaky being out here.

"There is nothing wrong with being crazy about life, Michael."

No I suppose not!

"I call it passion, my friend," He yelled and then proceeded to howl like a wolf at the moon.

You have a definite zest for life!

"Guilty as charged," Tom admitted as we both laughed hysterically for several minutes.

The waves were enormous that morning. The wind ferocious!

"Let me warn you, Michael, it is very rough out there today."

I signaled two thumbs up. No problem! I grew up in Hawaii! Remember?

"How could I forget?" Tom yelled over the gusting wind.

Lets go get wet shall we!

And off we went. Surfing in large swells was nothing compared to repelling a hundred and fifty foot waterfall! At least the fear it created in my mind was far more tame to a certain degree when it came to surfing. Unfortunately, the physical part of me didn't agree after being tossed around by the forces of Mother Nature that morning. I knew I would get beat up but I vowed to change my mental outlook on things no matter what.

When we arrived at the breaking point we sat for a few moments amongst the swells lit only by a touch of moonlight. Much of our surfing today would come from listening and feeling the waves due to the intense darkness.

"You know, passion guides your life," Tom said. "It has the ability to navigate you in the right direction."

I can see that when I look at you, Tom.

"It's the boost that gets me up in the morning to surf out here," Tom shouted in joy.

Also very early I will admit.

"Passion comes from your heart, Michael! And I want you to find it," he said.

Does that come when you give of yourself?

"When you embrace the bigger picture, Michael!"

What bigger picture are you referring too?

"That the deepest need for your heart, in connection with your soul is the need to live for something greater."

So you must be referring to your life purpose?

"Right! We are all here for a reason, remember, Michael," Tom replied.

I think of it as my future ambitions! I replied in confidence.

"There is no doubt in my mind that purpose provides you with passion and the compelling cause to motivate your journey in life, Michael."

How come you didn't mention goals or ambitions, Tom?

"Goals are fine if kept in context! Only if they come from the heart."

Ah! That darned mind again! I admitted.

"Motivating yourself with goals can be extremely fun but don't get lost in the translation, Michael! Goals usually entail physical items. And we both know where the desires of material come from! The ego! Your mind!"

Formulated from your beliefs, thoughts and imagination! What is truly wrong with that?

"Nothing! Nothing at all!" Tom exclaimed. "Using your mind is a wonderful thing if used appropriately."

So what's the problem? I inquired.

"Well you see its twofold, Michael! First off, goals a lot of the time become based on societies expectations and it doesn't take them long to become yours also. When the objects of your desire become strong enough your ego forces you to sacrifice your values, principles and integrity to get what it wants."

You mean becoming something we are not!

"Secondly, goals of the mind fade with your beliefs of what is possible or impossible."

Meaning we seldom follow through in reaching our goals.

"Precisely, Michael! Simply because your passion is based on the tangibles! That is why it is so important to manage your life with your heart instead of your mind."

The heart doesn't have to decipher between possible or impossible does it, Tom?

"No, the heart gives no consideration to what is impossible because everything is possible as far as it knows, Michael!"

The heart truly understands what's important!

"No, by living in your heart you truly understand what is important because your real self has a voice there. You live best in your heart, Michael."

I see your point! I admitted.

"You will when you understand the passion it brings you in relation to your life purpose," Tom shouted with excitement.

You must mean the intangibles?

"Yes, Michael! The intangibles!" Tom yelled through the wind. "You see tangible items like money, career, titles and material can be an absolute blast when kept in perspective."

What perspective are you referring too?

"The tangibles can provide you with the extra boost that adds fun to your life. Sparking an additional bit of passion regarding what you do."

So I don't see the problem then I am afraid.

"The problem is that society has placed great emphasis on these tangibles to define success, Michael."

Yes! You are right I suppose. They seem to be the measure of success or failure.

"Well, we both know that driving a BMW can be a whole ton of fun but you are neither a success or a failure if you have one or not. After all you cannot take items such as these with you when you leave the world through death can you, Michael?"

No, they stay behind when you leave! I replied.

"So my point is that instead of being passionate about balancing your life from the eight cornerstones that we express in, people become caught up in obsessing about the tangible items. Your true expression gets lost in the shuffle."

Does that mean your passion becomes your obsession and hence your destruction?

"Its all fun until the perspective is lost! Far too many people define themselves based on attaining these material items, Michael."

I suppose that your passion becomes your work at that point, Tom!

"I don't know, Michael, you tell me?" Tom replied.

Without an argument, it is definitely hard work! I admitted.

"Yes, even more so because you have to struggle to keep your life from collapsing around you."

Is that because the balance is lost?

"Again, you already know the answer, Michael, to that question," Tom replied.

Yes, I did destroy any sense of balance in my life and look where it got me.

"Remember, it is the lost connection with your spirit that has left you less connected to the world you are occupying for the moment. That is why you feel empty, confused about which direction to travel."

So the real passion gets lost in the illusions that cloud our better judgment, Tom?

"The real passion in you comes when you connect with your soul. Your heart is so much closer to your true self."

It's scary and exciting at the same time to hear that, I said.

Tom placed his hand on my shoulder. "Its passion when you understand your real purpose in life, Michael."

And most people are blinded to it due to the disconnection?

"Sure they are! When you finally connect with your soul you are real, doing what you were put on earth to do. Expressing your self in the eight cornerstones by giving a piece of your spirit to each. In return the universe provides for you everything that you need to survive."

So it is almost like a sequence of events?

"You could call it something like that I suppose!" Tom remarked.

I pretended like I was making a sales pitch. Be, Do, Have is a very catchy formula wouldn't you admit, Tom?

"That is a viable formula for passion!" Tom yelled in that moment.

So it starts when your heart and soul converge as one.

"Now you are starting to see the bigger picture, Michael!"

Tom disappeared only to be seen at the apex of a gigantic wave that toppled over him as if he were out of his element. It appeared he was okay following the wipe out and now it was my turn. Off the point I saw a beauty of a giant. I paddled as hard as I could to catch it. Having been positioned accurately I made it in time to ride it a few feet before being thrust under its powerful spell. As a surfer you learn that when you fall off the wave you get right back on the board. We were off again thrashing in the waves before sunrise.

"You know Michael!" Tom said. "You are about to embark on leaving a life of default to entering one by design."

How so? I asked him intrigued by his statement.

"No more sleep walking through your life anymore."

I can already see that happening, I admitted to Tom.

"You have to know a couple of things that pertain to finding the real passion in life, Michael."

And I am confident you are going to share those with me, Tom.

"Michael, I want you to begin by keeping the promises that you make to not only others but to yourself."

I haven't had much success with keeping promises I am afraid.

"When you break them you will notice that tiny fragments of your heart shatter with each broken promise. Not only that, with each broken promise you slowly begin to dent your integrity, lowering your self esteem to the point that you section off pieces of your real self to the world."

I can understand that! That is exactly how I began my downward spiral.

"Keeping those promises builds confidence in your heart lending to the growth of your own personal power."

That alone must fuel your engine to live passionately. I can believe it is too easy to break promises when all you have to consider is yourself.

"Indeed it is, Michael," Tom replied. "However, I think you are beginning to see that life isn't about you directly."

Admittedly, each day I have been coming to know that.

"So that should already lead you to understanding exactly what you need to do. Great human beings don't do what is easiest, Michael! They do what is right!"

So doing what is right means keeping the promises I make with myself and to others?

"No, Michael! Keep the promises your heart makes within all of the eight cornerstones from which you live."

Does that mean avoid making promises with myself?

"Equalize the divisions of your self to balance the important areas with which you have the ability to contribute too. In doing so you will stay out of your head by paying honor to your heart."

We both looked up to the moon as the wind and waves whisked around our surfboards.

So what is the other facet of passion that I need to grasp, Tom.

"What are you most grateful for in your life? Tom questioned me on the spot.

I would have to say things like my career, money, status and health.

"Okay, so tell me how you honor that gratitude for life, Michael?"

By simply being grateful! I answered.

Tom was laughing. "Nice try wise guy! Do you actually channel your gratitude throughout the course of a typical day?"

I would never have time to do something like that, Tom.

"Well, that is what people who live from the heart do, Michael."

How?

"There are a number of ways to show your gratitude, Michael!"

Have you ever considered reflection, journaling or meditation as methods to capture these incredible moments that you have lived to experience?"

I can honestly say I have not!

"Take all the beautiful things, the people you have met and the places you have been. Begin to focus on them as we speak."

What for? Isn't that living in the past?

"No! When you focus on these extraordinary gifts you will experience a growth that becomes a part of your daily life. I am not asking you to relive these accounts but I am suggesting you honor their beauty, the power that the universe has supplied for you. By dwelling on all the beautiful energy that exists in them you will see an amazing thing happen."

And what might that be?

"What you dwell on becomes your reality. What you think about expands, Michael!"

That all comes from being grateful!

"It is a way to connect to the universe and thank it for all it has provided in your life."

And that's why you are in awe every time you see the sun, stand on the beach, surf in the ocean or watch a sunrise, Tom?

"Yes! I am just being grateful, even thankful of the perfection that exists in the universe," Tom mentioned.

I was smiling a bright smile amidst the darkness. I am beginning to understand the passion you are talking about! However, I consider your definition of passion to be much different from mine.

"There is only one true definition of passion, Michael!"

I can appreciate that! I replied.

"Its even better when you get to actually live it," Tom remarked.

The sun was starting to pierce its way through the darkness by revealing a hint of orange just over the horizon. I watched in my newfound appreciation for the world on my surfboard amidst the pounding waves.

"How do you want to be remembered when you leave life, Michael?"

Wow! That is a very deep question! I replied.

"I think it is a fair one to ask you with all things considered."

I have thought an awful lot about my success. You know my accomplishments in the business world.

"You mean you have been focused on the fame, fortune and celebrity of it all," Tom remarked.

Absolutely! I admitted.

"Wouldn't it be cool to do something other than for yourself that bordered on greatness, Michael?"

Like what, Tom?

"How about touching the hearts of others by sharing a piece of yours with them!" Tom shouted.

I nodded my head. Just like the way you have made a life out it!

"Precisely! But I am not the only example in the world, Michael."

You will be remembered for the creation of your revolutionary program at the center and by every person you were able to help, I said as if I were talking to myself out loud.

Tom took a modest tone. "That is my legacy! I want to know yours, Michael!"

I suppose I will need to construct some thought pertaining to mine, I admitted.

"Listen, Michael, you needn't hibernate for weeks on end in order to brainstorm an elaborate legacy!"

Oh! So how else will I consider it?

"By listening and responding to your heart. The place that lies closest to the true Michael Jamieson," Tom replied. "I created mine in response to waking up from the nightmare that overtook me. As a response to saying thank you to the world I hadn't truly seen before."

A way to express your gratitude!

"In reality the world has provided me with so much that I strive to give back a piece of my inner spirit to it every single day in some way, shape or form," Tom shouted.

Your purpose! I stated as if to finally see a bigger scope in front of me.

"You can do it too, Michael! In fact, I encourage you to live that way."

Learn to appreciate it all just as you have done, Tom?

"Sure! What else can you do? Don't you think it would be a shame for you to die like you almost did several weeks ago without having won a victory for the world?"

That is how you will be remembered! For your victories, Tom!

"I see you being remembered in that very same fashion, Michael, I honestly do!"

You do! I said surprised at the idea.

"However, to transform your life you have to first transform yourself."

You are referring to the answers that are within!

Tom paddled off once again to ride another offering from the universe. We surfed until well into the morning hours. A combination of surfing and talking about the topic of passion! I was awestruck by my experience with Tom up to that point. So much in fact, that I had missed out on the many beautiful experiences he had been showing me all along. However, I would not let that morning become a part of my previous ignorance. I was bound and determined that it was all on the brink of change.

I truly had the understanding of why Tom appeared to be so different from many of us. His persistent grin, the ridiculous clichés, the early morning surfing, his connection to the outdoors and his remarkable program! These were all connections he had formulated stemming from his real self-passion with that of the physical world. It was all expressed in perfect harmony. Tom's passion was in everything he did, touched or said. Everything! It was only now that I had finally begun to take notice of how he also wanted me to express my life. With real unobstructed passion!

Reflection

"Life is not measured by the number of breaths we take,
but by the moments that take our breath away."
-George Carlin-

After, Lisa and I had parted ways I remember a night in particular where I had returned home to discover a large box that was left behind. In it were countless photographs that had been captured over our many years together.

I rummaged through pictures of our college days. Our adventures to Hawaii, Europe and China! I relived moments from our wedding day, holiday celebrations, birthdays and even the birth of our daughter. It was all in that lone box. The years of my life with family and friends! It was a surprising trip down old memory lane but a sad one nonetheless when I looked back at what I had left behind.

Most of these images I had forgotten. Being so wrapped up in oneself I think it makes it easy to play ignorant to the world around you. However, I was glad the box was left in my possession as it sparked some appreciation for the many great years in my life that I had been fortunate enough to experience. Not only that the images rekindled the haunting doubts I still had about leaving a part of my life behind.

Together, Lisa and I graduated from college and fell madly in love. We spent countless days together just being ourselves. Walking along the many miles of beach on the California coastline. Surfing together in Hawaii. Scuba diving in Australia and standing at the top of the Eiffel Tower in Paris! Over the years we were fortunate to touch the Buddha in Hong Kong, see many a sunset in Monterey and ski the slopes of the Rocky Mountains. During all of these moments I remember confessing our love for each other until we finally stood at the alter on our wedding day to honor it.

During my race through the years gone by I felt grateful for the experience of bringing a daughter into the world. I cherished the memories of my family, friends and loved ones. However, the void I felt the most was the absence of the abundant love that at one time not so long ago filled the halls of the massive mansion I slept in. At one time it was fueled by the dreams in Lisa's heart and the love of our family when our daughter entered our lives.

There was no denying that my life had encompassed some of the most memorable moments known to man. Moments in theory I wouldn't trade for anything in the world. But did! Experiences that I should have cherished and honored for the rest of my life.

Moments that I had forgotten! Who could forget events and images like these I thought to myself? For most people images like these occupy a large portion of their long-term memory. But I had no recollection for the "good" in my past until that night alone with the box. And even after reminiscing I only held the "good" in my head for a short period before letting it adrift as if it was that of an estranged life.

When most people would be tremendously satisfied, I was frustrated. When most would be at peace with their decisions, I was in conflict. You see these were the things that mattered in the lives of most. Things like family, children, loved ones and the events that come with being involved with a life of such. The truly important aspects of life you could say. However, for me they didn't seem to matter with any great importance. At least at the time or I would have never have left it all behind.

I so ignorantly gave up the most prestigious items of value that any person on earth would strive to achieve. Believing that I was all that mattered in the world I threw it all away to travel my journey alone. Hoping somewhere along the way that I would find the key to unlock the happiness I lacked!

With so desperately wanting to be at peace with myself, longing to love the person I had become, I turned my back on all that actually made me happy. Instead, I became an image larger than life in my own perverse way. I gave up my passion for life for my obsession in the boardroom! I defecated on the happiness that did exist when I separated from my wife and daughter! I spit in the face of the universe and all that it provided by continuing the search for the unknowns that I feared. I should have opened my eyes somewhere along the way to see the same images that I leafed through that night in the box.

I realized in those moments that there is a lot to sacrifice when you decide to give up life in the present by resigning to the unknowns of the future and taking solace in the past. The search I initiated by examining my past and hoping to find refuge in the future never finished nor did the pain. I suppose the most hurtful reality of it all was my realization as to why I chose to sacrifice my present life at all. A question that has remained without an obvious answer for a large part of my pathetic existence!

Chapter Twelve:
The Seventh Day in May:
The Power of Thoughts

"Strength of numbers is the delight of the timid.
The valiant in spirit glory in fighting alone."
-Mohandas Koramchand Gandhi-

That afternoon I met Tom on the south side lawn of the center property. Upon my arrival I could see a sleek, black, jet helicopter parked on the grass. Tom was standing next to it talking with the pilot. As I approached them Tom openly greeted me as he introduced me to his friend, Charlie. Tom explained that Charlie had flown helicopter missions in Kuwait and Somalia before lending his piloting skills to the commercial crafts of corporate America. Today, however, Charlie would be chauffeuring the skies with Tom and I aboard his chopper. I was excited because I had never flown in a helicopter before even though I had access to the company bird whenever I needed. It would prove to be yet another exciting first for me during my days with Tom.

As the pilot engaged the engine, Tom and I boarded the helicopter and dawned the headsets to accommodate communication while in flight.

"You are in for a real treat this afternoon," Tom shouted over the noisy engine.

Where are we heading?

"Well, I would imagine Charlie is going to marvel you with the skies over destination unknown, my friend. It won't be disappointing!"

No, I wouldn't think so!

"I would guess that we will tour the coast before heading over the air space of the charming city of San Francisco."

Wild! I replied.

I was staring out the window of the helicopter awaiting our take off.

"The last little while has been very new and no doubt adventurous for you, Michael!"

More like turbulent, Tom!

"Well, your life is only what you think it is," Tom replied.

I have a tough time buying that comment coach!

Next the helicopter began its take off, rising and hovering through the air. Charlie lifted us straight off the ground with absolute ease to about a hundred feet. It was at that point when I could see that we had made a full rotation to face the ocean. With ease the chopper made a very slow motion in the direction of the blue water when Charlie came over the cabin radio reminding us to buckle up. In that instant, Charlie hit full throttle and I could feel the jets engage in a thrusting force. It was like riding a roller coaster. At first my stomach sank before flying forward in my abdominal cavity. There was no speed limit to my knowledge in these friendly skies and we must have been flying full out. It was beautiful as we headed down the coast over the calm waters of the Pacific Ocean. It was a great day to fly and it proved to be just that as the scenery from above was awesome.

As we admired the view Tom broke the silence of the helicopter engine.

"There is something truly important that you are not quite coming to grips with, Michael."

Oh! What would you say that is?

"Transforming your life is a consciousness. Growth is a consciousness. Connecting to your heart and your inner power is a consciousness. Propelling your life to newer and higher levels of awareness is a consciousness."

So what your saying is that hoping, praying and wishing for a life changing experience isn't going to happen for me?

"No, as a matter of fact it won't because you have to be the transformation before you can make the transformation," Tom replied.

As we discussed before I know I have the power to control my life.

"Yes you do! And you also have the power to control your thoughts. I want you to begin taking advantage of putting the power of your thoughts to work for you, Michael!"

I must admit that I am trying the best I can.

"You also know that fear is a consciousness, self-pity is a consciousness."

I interrupted Tom. Okay, stop it right there!

"That is how you have been leading your life whether you want to hear it or not."

That is precisely why I am trying to take the proper measures to redirect my life.

"Well, if your going to accomplish that than you better understand that it begins with your thoughts," Tom shouted over the noise of the engine.

Say what?

"You have a magnetic capability that I don't think you consciously have been acknowledging, Michael."

What kind of capability are you talking about?

"The connection between your heart and your mind is what I am talking about."

You told me to live only from the heart! I exclaimed.

"I told you to live more so from your heart with less emphasis in your mind. The mind and the heart have a connection. Except most people believe them to be separate entities. Together the two are an extremely powerful resource of energy for you to use when you involve your soul."

So you are saying that I cannot live fully from the heart alone?

"Not if you expect to show the world the real you, Michael. The strongest connection exists between your head and your heart as guided by your inner power!"

So it's a balanced flow between these two mediums?

"You see, their must be a proper allocation of the time spent between your heart and that in your mind. However, society doesn't practice like that, Michael."

No, the focus usually encompasses being lost in your head!

"Right! People are stifled by the power of the mind in dominating their thoughts."

And that must be why so many people have lost the connection with their inner power, Tom.

"Yes! We have discussed at great length that the mind is chasing the elusive expectations dreamed up by others."

I remember that! I replied.

"Together, the heart and the mind have the ability to collaborate. Enabling them to filter the ego dominated thoughts we have attracted in relation to people, places and things. Therefore, reaching a state of harmony in executing the expression of your inner power in life."

That's a very deep concept!

"Okay, here is a little chemistry and physiology lesson for you my student," Tom said with a smile. "Take a recurring thought that you have been experiencing like doubting you will ever reconcile with your wife. Now, take it to your subconscious mind, Michael."

No problem! That is what I have been doing already it seems.

"I know!" Tom replied. "So what does that do?"

I can't answer the question just yet I am only the student remember!

"It vibrates to your inner power and adjoins with your innate intelligence, your soul, within you."

Sarcastically, I frowned at Tom. So what?

"Your thoughts, add color to your soul and it is those colors that become your reality, Michael."

Let me think about it for a minute! You are saying that my thoughts repeated over and over pass to the subconscious mind which in turn translates into my physical reality?

"You got it!" Tom applauded me. "Your thoughts both positive and negative are made up of energy. In your case the negative thoughts are repeatedly recycled in your mind resulting in becoming your physical reality."

So obviously thoughts are incredibly powerful!

"Without a doubt, Michael! Focus your thoughts on what you don't want in your life and what you don't want winds up becoming the physical equivalent."

Does the same theory apply to positive thoughts, Tom?

"Yes it does! That is why it is so important to direct your thoughts to what it is you do want in your life!"

If positive thoughts predominate than they can become real? Right!

"They certainly can, Michael! It is a consciousness we're talking about. By understanding the connection between your heart and your head the clarity of your soul allows your dominating thoughts to become your reality for the betterment of your life."

The conversation took a brief pause. It was all fascinating stuff I thought as we both continued to soak in the scenery from above the city of San Francisco.

"When you sit in your room at night wishing and doubting at the same time in relation to changing your life direction your mind clearly overshadows your heart."

And those wishes and doubts are the same things that I am running from!

They have the likelihood of becoming real?

"They have the potential to hold you back! To keep you from growing as a person, Michael."

How so? I asked Tom.

"Sometimes there can be an interference between the head and the heart that prevents the true you from commandeering your thought processes in a conscious manner. When it occurs, the mind hands over the command post to the ego instead of your soul. As we already understand the ego tends to run from what it fears instead of towards what your heart actually knows. In the end the fear of your ego cannot outrun itself and you end up with what you were trying to avoid in the first place."

So then what?

"It becomes a lifestyle you wind up living with, Michael!"

So is that why the heart is considered to be the superior manager in my life direction?

"The heart is much closer to your soul. It's the medium to express your real self and it knows what is right, Michael!"

So what about the mind?

"It is a blend of conscious versus the subconscious. The conscious end is comprised of your thoughts, ideas and imagination."

So what about the subconscious? I asked further.

"The subconscious is the inspiration, the action based on what is right and that comes from your heart. All of your thoughts, negative and positive are attached to an emotion that is also positive or negative."

Do these emotions offer us some kind of action plan?

"Precisely! That is what brings them to reality!" Tom exclaimed.

So when I punish myself for my actions, worry about never seeing my family or stew about how to change my life direction I am focusing on more of what is already a reality in the present?

"And that is why you believe that your life will be impossible to transform, Michael!"

You are totally right! I replied.

"Can you see the funk you are in?"

I do, I admitted.

Looking out the window of the helicopter I surrendered to the fact that I had been living with my eyes closed. Once again, Tom had helped me open them. It was ridiculous because I remembered a few days previous when we met and I told Tom that I believed I had the power to control my thoughts. It seemed as though I relinquished any control I had assumed, only to tell Tom what I believed he wanted to hear. In doing so I failed to listen to my own inner voice. Again, I witnessed the captivating powers that prevailed in blocking my soul its rightful expression in my life.

"Michael, you no doubt have the conscious ability to control your thoughts. By now you should also understand the rules of what does and doesn't work."

It appears as though it boils down to consciousness, I admitted.

"And you are going to get there," Tom replied.

I guess it will require some continuous construction.

"Absolutely, Michael!" Tom shouted with excitement. "Happiness, success, fear, failure, doubt are all thoughts at one time or another you will come to experience. The difference is when you establish a conscious connection between your heart and your head. Then and only then will you be equipped with the consciousness necessary to decipher which thoughts will actually become your reality. Consciousness is a knowing. It is a reality and when you lend consciousness to your thoughts both positive and negative you offer them a sense of knowing. And what you know has the capacity to become real."

I appeared frustrated. I want it all to change, Tom!

"If that be the case than know one thing, Michael! Every positive thought you have about what it is you want for your life carries with it the seed of an equivalent action."

I see the emphasis you placed on a big enough why during our last meeting! I said in disbelief.

"When it becomes your consciousness, you will know that your heart and head are once again in sync with each other. Then you will encounter the reality generated from your soul."

I am what I think I am! I stated laughing.

Tom was very serious despite my attempt at humor.

"Funny or not it is very true, Michael! To put in other words, just a half-month away from the Ides of June, it is tempting to borrow that time honored quote from Shakespeare's 'Julius Caesar'. "The fault dear Brutus is not in our stars but in ourselves, that we are underlings." I have learned that there is no such thing as fear, doubt, and failure! Only what you decide to create in your mind, Michael!"

The mind I am learning is a very powerful place, I replied.

"It is a place where most people's familiarity exists. Don't let that familiarity become your life again, Michael. Know that consciously nothing exists unless you create it first in your mind. Run toward that which your heart demands and stop running from what your head fears. And when you do you will find the answers pertaining to the reality of what your true life is capable of becoming."

I have to remember that I have the power inside to make it all become a reality, Tom.

"That is the power of thought, right there, Michael! You see the wheels are already in motion. Now enjoy the ride!"

Reflection

"Do or do not—There is no try."
-Yoda-

They are the misfits, the crazy ones
The round pegs in the square holes
The ones who see things differently.
They are not fond of rules and
They have no respect for status quo.

You can quote them, disagree with them,
Glorify or vilify them.
The only thing you can't do is ignore them.
Because they change things
They push the human race forward
And some may see them as the crazy ones
We see genius.

Because the people who are crazy enough
To think they can change the world
Are the ones who do.

-Unknown-

Chapter Thirteen:
The Eighth Day in May:
Your Last Day On Earth

"Someday, after we have mastered the winds, the waves, the tide and gravity,
we shall harness for God the energies of love. Then, for the second time
in the history of the world, man will have discovered fire."
-Pierre Teilhard De Chardin-

It was the last day in May, which for me represented my final meeting with my life coach, Tom. Furthermore, it was also my last day of the program at the center. I was set to graduate with the knowledge to help me stay free and clear of drugs and alcohol. However, I had one final lesson to learn from Tom. I had assumed that after the last meeting I would be well equipped to further my already progressing personal development. At Tom's request I met him in the center's courtyard that afternoon. When I arrived he was his usual jovial self as he sat waiting atop an outdoor bench in the sun, humming a happy tune.

"Today represents our last day in May, Michael!"

Yes it does! I replied with a discouraged tone. I find it quite sad that our friendship has to end.

"Who said anything about ending?"

I just assumed that since my month and a half here at the center was complete that our time together would also conclude.

"Michael, today is no doubt a monumental moment in your life but it is certainly one that we will continue to foster outside of the centers program."

It is comforting to know that my incredible experience will continue beyond today, Tom. But I would hardly describe the moment as "monumental."

"You came to the center as a empty spirit without direction. You isolated yourself in search of important answers to solve it. You fought off death but succumbed to the dangers of drugs and alcohol in the end."

Please, lets leave the life summary alone for now! I pleaded.

"Compared to when you walked into to my place here I would have to say that it is a monumental occasion in your life, Michael!"

Well, I will admit that it has definitely been life changing, the experience that is.

"The counselors tell me you have made a complete 180 degree turn in your mental outlook and your health."

And what do you think of that, Tom?

"I would agree with them Michael," He replied.

You would? I said surprised. Do you think I am ready for the real world?

"Look at you! You are in great physical shape. You have combated the desire to return to a previous chemical dependency. The psychological staff marvels at your ability to have survived even your past alone. Professionally, I would coin you a survivor, Mr. Jamieson," Tom shouted proudly.

I managed to force a smirk not fully welcoming the title of survivor. I guess I am!

"You should be extremely proud of that, Michael!"

I never really looked at it in that context before, I admitted.

Tom barked at me. "Of course you didn't Michael! Simply because you have never consciously seen your life until now!"

Say that once again for me, Tom?

"The look in your eyes that I see now is so much different from the look you had when you arrived here to the center, Michael."

How so? I asked.

"Before I saw the outline of Michael Jamieson, a man that disconnected from his real self. When I looked into your eyes I saw your soul trapped inside your body. In place of your inner power I saw the anger of the broken soul you had become."

You were able to see all of that from my eyes alone?

"You made it easy for me, Michael. However, to hide from your misdirection you turned to drugs and alcohol."

Your assessment is completely accurate, once again.

"Today is a different story, Michael! I am not here today to remind you of your past."

What is so different now as you see it?

"In front of me I can see your soul in plain sight and I know that you have reconnected with it. My only hope is that you continue to foster the connection between your heart and your mind for the long-term."

Really! I said shocked at Tom's words.

"The evolution of the real you is already beginning, Michael!"

I sense a tremendous presence inside my former empty body. I would call it a feeling of inner peace or content.

Tom offered a smile. "That is precisely what happens when you have all the tools to open the door to living from the heart."

You believe I have all the tools now, Tom? I replied.

We took a moment in silence following my question. It was as if Tom ignored my need to seek his reinforcement.

I felt the need to confess. Before I attempted to put my faith in the hands of someone else hoping that they could change my life direction for me!

"All of that has changed, Michael!"

Yes it has! I realize now that the only person capable of transforming my life is "me".

"You are referring to the energy that lights up your life!"

Instead of worrying about the disasters I had been living through, I have come to know that my life isn't truly even about my own selfishness.

Tom reinforced my words. "It's about the universe around you, Michael, and what you have to offer it."

Yes, I finally understand! That is what you have been terming the 'bigger picture'.

"I am confident that you are well on your way through the next chapter of your life, Michael."

I know it has already begun, I replied.

"You are an incredible energy!" Tom said. "Taking flight on an unbelievable journey!"

I paused for a moment. Thank you, I think?

"I see a power on the brink of greatness! Just remember what you have to offer the world, Michael."

I can only hope to follow in your footsteps, Tom, I replied.

"You are fully conscious beyond what the average man acquaints with. It is refreshing to watch you allow your inner spirit the opportunity to shine through to those around you."

I certainly had my doubts when we started, I admitted.

"Sure you did, Michael. You thought you were coming here to get clean so you could get your job back."

That's right! My former self had offered me no other choice, I said.

"Instead you can now see the invitation from Dr. Marshall for what it truly was."

Yes! It was a message from the universe that I couldn't see because of the rather dark cloud looming overhead at the time.

"Aren't you glad you trusted yourself enough to follow Dr. Marshall's lead?"

It was the first perceived risk of the many more I intend to take in my life, Tom!

"You will prosper beyond your wildest imagination from your commitment to be your real self, Michael! Just you wait and see. Everything you truly are will rain down on the world and in return the universe will provide you with everything you need to continue your journey."

I had a look of surprise on my face. It will, Tom?

"Without a doubt, Michael!"

"Remember, Michael! The place where you have feared the most is also where your greatest growth lies."

I remember hearing you say that the other day when we met.

"I am glad to see that you are starting to understand that the easiest way to live your life is to just be yourself."

I blew a sighing breath of air. I am trying to let my heart dominate!

"I can see that!" Tom stated. "However, there is no such thing as trying, Michael!"

"Really?"

"Absolutely! 'Trying' is nothing more than a money back guarantee that people cast as an illusion to go all out with their lives. I don't want to see you do that with the new found wealth that you have come upon."

So the illusion of 'trying' is a lie that we make to ourselves?

"It's a half-hearted approach that we implement towards the things that cross our life path. The problem is that 'trying' is nothing more than a lost cause from the outset."

I am a little confused, Tom!

"Okay, I want you to stand up from where you are sitting, Michael."

I stood up in front of Tom. So now what?

"Take a seat again, Michael!" Tom directed. "Now, 'try' to stand up again."

I stood up in front of the chair as Tom had requested. So what?

"Well, for starters I asked you to 'try' and you are actually standing in front

179

of the chair. I didn't ask you to stand, Michael! I requested you 'try'."

Oh! I see, I admitted. 'Trying' only confuses your innate power within because you cannot try and actually accomplish something at the same time.

"Right, Michael! I couldn't have said it any better myself. You either commit to something or not. But you should never 'try'!"

I completely understand, now.

"Remember, you can't get wet by saying the word water, Michael. You have to jump into that ocean of an inner being inside of your heart first if you want to transition your life."

What you are saying feels right on the inside, Tom!

"Life is risky! You have to take those risks to avoid regret."

It sounds like an avenue to achieve freedom.

"Do the one thing daily that makes you terrified, Michael! On the other side of your fear is the freedom you have been searching for."

I suppose I just need to continue strategizing without my head?

"Listen more with your heart instead of 'trying' with your mind. The heart will not mislead you. It will only commit."

The multiple rings of Tom's mobile phone interrupted us! He excused himself from our conversation by mentioning that it was an important call he needed to address. The break in our deep discussion was a welcoming moment for me. It gave me the opportunity to express my gratitude to the universe for enabling me to have traveled to the center. It was a journey that I was reluctant to engage but all things considered the beginning of a much larger transformation to uncover the answers I had been desperately searching for. To ultimately change my life!

I had finally been able to acknowledge who I truly was. Beginning to express it to the physical world. From that moment on, it was going to be me who would be directing the life that I had intended to live. Especially, after learning the many insights from my meetings with Tom. Lessons he provided as a framework to continue my journey on the inside instead of the spiraling cycle of events I had become entrenched in on the outside. Strategies to carve a new path both inside and out were starting to come to fruition. You could call it a 'new beginning' of sorts.

Tom returned from his phone call with resurgence in his words.

"Your consciousness has arrived and I want you to embrace the transformation you have made from the moth you use to be to the butterfly you are destined to become, Michael."

I actually feel incredibly different.

"The process is well under way," Tom replied.

I am sure it won't be easy but at least I will consciously commit to sticking to it.

"Interestingly enough you mention the work it will take to continue on your path, Michael!"

What do you mean? I asked.

"Consciousness isn't something you have to work at. It either becomes you or it doesn't. Remember it is a knowing that resides from your heart when you live there. Now you have it, so I doubt very much you will ever lose it again."

In a reluctant tone I responded, Okay!

"Maybe I can offer you one last little tidbit of information that can help you to maintain your balanced connection," Tom mentioned.

Sure anything to help!

"Michael, if I diagnosed you with a terminal disease, giving you one month to live what would you do knowing what you now know?"

I suppose I would visit the people and the places in my life that at one time mattered the most to me. Perhaps tell them how I truly feel! Even spend meaningful moments in their presence. I may even embark on a few risky adventures myself if I knew I was going to die.

"So why wouldn't you consider living everyday of your remaining time in that capacity?"

I was speechless. For the first time in my life I had nothing to say, not even a sarcastic remark.

"You already know that you never actually die. Remember your energy when it leaves the physical world through perceived death takes on a different form. It is infinite!"

I remember, Tom!

"So again, I ask why not live everyday as if it were your very last on earth?"

You are right! Why not! I replied.

"Just think how easy it would be for you to stay connected to your inner power enabling the world to witness the 'real you' by giving of yourself to your fullest potential," Tom shouted in excitement.

I suppose you wouldn't leave anything behind!

"And you shouldn't!" Tom stated. "Can you imagine the power of telling the people around you how you actually feel? Saying or doing the things you have always dared to do but held back in keeping them bottled up inside."

No more fearing the expression of the 'real me'! I said in determination.

"Do the things you have always known you have wanted to do, Michael! See

181

the beauty the world has to offer! Accomplish the tasks you have been putting off and the ones you never thought possible. Taking risks is something too few people in the universe choose to do because they are afraid."

Tom took a very serious tone in that moment. "That is what I mean when I say live like today was your very last day!"

You live your life in that capacity also! I said. I can see it now!

"As I have said before I experienced firsthand what living a life of unconsciousness can do. So I chose to consciously live more from my heart each day letting my innate self come through."

And it does!

"I listen to my heart. It tells me what is right! I say what I feel! I share myself with everyone around me no matter what. I am so thankful for the perfection that I am a part of and what the whole physical life experience has to offer. I am in awe of the beauty around us. Passionate about my purpose and each moment I spend awake I will continue to champion victories for mankind by offering a piece of myself to the world. Most importantly I have a blast being able to do what I do!"

I have seen in my time at the center everything you have just described about how you live your life. The worst part is that I didn't recognize it until now!

"Live each day as if it were your last, Michael! It is so much easier to appreciate the connection with your inner self, your soul, when you do! And when you live like it is your last day on earth your fear subsides in the love that emanates from your innate spirit. Your passion will soar and your purpose will shine. Above all else you will not have any regrets to torture yourself with any longer."

I couldn't help but sound surprised. No regrets at all?

"No, because you will act on your life in ways you would never think otherwise," Tom shouted confidently."

No more holding back! I stated in a revelation.

"Don't become another one of those lost spirits chasing after the elusive image of success."

Already been there and done that, as you know, Tom!

"And you already know it will only cause you to lose perspective of the balance in your life, Michael!"

You mean it will topple the balance within the eight cornerstones of my life?

"The balance can be lost when you are trapped in the mind."

So the connection with your heart becomes unbalanced also!

"Yes! It has the potential to prevent you from saying and doing the things in your life until it is perhaps too late."

You mean death?

"It could be death, injury or illness. Whatever the scenario it usually holds you back from offering the pieces of yourself and your heart that were designed to be expressed in the cornerstones you live from. All growth and transformation comes to a screeching halt."

I guess that is the time where most people wish they had the chance to say the important words or see the beautiful sights when they had the chance!

Tom pointed at me. "All I can tell you, Michael, is to not become one of those people. One day when you are on your deathbed never for a second wish your life was different. Don't for a minute wish to have it back!"

Go full out now? Right!

"Give of yourself 100% today! Your optimal potential! It's all you have, Michael. The human experience flies by so fast that it would be a shame for it to not be what it absolutely was destined to be!"

I won't argue the issue of time.

"You are here as a spiritual being having a human experience. It is a gift! Something that you must celebrate while you are here, Michael."

Any given day could be your last I suppose.

"Don't let it be, Michael! Give your life everything you have, every single day. Don't hold back. Then you can begin each consecutive day after these, if you are fortunate enough to do so, as a new beginning."

It would be amazing to start off everyday free and clear from the next.

"Think about the feeling you would get from everyday being a new day in a new world!"

You are absolutely right! I admitted. It would be incredibly powerful.

"It would also be incredibly fun wouldn't you agree," Tom shouted with a smile.

I was grinning from ear to ear. I can envision a life bursting with passion!

"All you have to do is become comfortable enough to trust your heart and take those dares in your everyday life."

Become comfortable enough to do the uncomfortable things!

"It will guarantee the connection of your spiritual energy and your heart, Michael."

Will that help maintain my connection with my spiritual energy?

"Remember Michael! To transform your life you must transform first."

Right! I guess I just get so enthused that I tend to get ahead of myself, I admitted.

"The grandest illusion of mankind is the fear of the unknown, Michael!"

The unknown doesn't actually exist when you put your heart in the hands of the universe, I replied.

"Yes, Michael! The universe in all of its perfection if you trust it will shower you with the abundance it has to offer. When you have reached a consciousness like you have, you will always understand that you will never want for anything ever again."

The only unknown is that created in the mind, I concluded.

"Yes! And that fear is the greatest fear of the ego. To just reveal your innate power, your spirit, your soul to the world!"

Our greatest fear is in just being ourselves.

"So just be yourself anyway and trust the universe!" Tom replied.

That's a commitment I intend to make with myself!

"Remember it is a whole lot easier to solidify that connection when you live each day like it was your last."

I looked at Tom and smiled. Live like I was dying! I repeated.

"Live like you were dying!" Tom shouted with excitement.

"Now you have all the tools in your tool box, Michael! You are more than ready to take on the world."

Thank you for everything, I replied.

"Don't for a minute thank me for anything. The answers you have found in our meetings over the last month are the answers that were deeply entrenched inside of your heart."

Smoke and mirrors darkened the way I suppose! I replied. Well, your guidance has been much appreciated during my stay, Tom!

"Again, all I did was act to interrupt your current life course with several key applications to help you plot a new life journey," Tom admitted humbly.

Just an interruption, huh!

"It was only an interruption that was needed to put your current life travels on hold and offer you the opportunity to see something you had never seen before, Michael. In the process the real Michael Jamieson has awakened to the world."

Yes, the whole experience can really be coined an awakening for me! I admitted.

"You are destined for many amazing things, Michael!" Tom confessed.

"Let your soul lead you through your heart. Grab hold of that connection! Feel it's power and live with it each and every day. Never let go my friend!" Tom yelled with enthusiasm.

I will never let go, Tom!

It was at that moment I realized that the journey called "My Life" had already begun to travel in a different direction. Except on that day I was able to see that it was happening. Tom stood up in front of me and offered me a giant hug before asking me to accompany him to a special meeting he had to attend. Of course I would oblige his invitation. Tom had never given me any reason to doubt him! So I wasn't about to start now. I placed my trust in the universe thus far and Tom had helped to clear my vision to see it. Happy but sad at the same time I accompanied my new found mentor and friend down the west corridor of the center. I felt at peace with my life for the first time ever. It was the very thing I had been searching for all the time I had been destroying my life in the process. It was a powerful consciousness that I had learned to employ, as I was ready and waiting for whatever entered my latest journey.

Reflection

"The great end in life is not knowledge but action."
-Thomas Henry Huxley-

I remembered a passage that was read during the funeral proceedings of my brother. I felt that during my present journey they tweaked the heartstrings of my former life. Furthermore, the passage represents the discovery that is waiting for all of us if we choose to initiate the fulfilling journey within.

If, as Herod, we fill our lives with things, and again with thing;
If we consider ourselves so unimportant that we must fill every
Moment of our lives with action, when will we have the time to make the
long, slow journey across the desert as did the Magi? Or sit and watch the
stars as did the Shepards? Or brood over the coming of the child as did Mary?
For each one of us, there is a desert to travel. And a star to discover.
And a being within ourselves to bring to life."

-Unknown-

Chapter Fourteen:
The Last Day in May:
A New Beginning

"We must be willing to get rid of the life we've planned,
so as to have the life that is waiting for us."
-Joseph Campbell-

As Tom and I traveled down the sun drenched west corridor of the center it appeared as though we were headed in the direction of the guest lounge. Although I felt a deep sense of inner peace in my heart I was bursting with anticipation as to whom I was suppose to meet.

The interaction between the two of us on the walk was non-existent! In fact, there was no conversation. No discussion. No talking at all! Tom seemed to fit the mold of the proverbial 'Man on a Mission'. He had a purpose in that time. Instead of his joyful, jovial self he was focused on reaching our destination. Just before we reached the guest lounge Tom changed it all when he decided to come to a screeching halt.

"Michael! I have said it to you already and I will say it again. You are now ready to take your life and turn it into something that is absolutely extra-ordinary!"

It feels as though the timing couldn't be better, I replied.

"The pieces are finally in place for you!"

I understand!

"I want you to know that not only are the pieces in order, Michael, but so are you. You see you are the main player in the game of life!"

I had a confused look on my face. The player? What game?

"Come with me. It is time to test the inner connection you have made, Michael!"

Wait a second, I want to know about the players! I said confused by the notion.

Tom wore a warm smile on his face. "Follow me and it will all fall in to place, Michael."

Confused by Tom's words I was reluctant to oppose the man who helped to guide me through the chaos that comprised my life. Together we entered the guest lounge to watch as the answers to my questions were revealed. The room itself was showered with the full radiant sunlight from the afternoon. The windows had been opened enabling a fresh breeze to warm the area. There were many people scattered throughout the lounge because it represented a graduation day of sorts to the programs attendees. It marked the beginning of a new chapter on a newfound journey for all of us.

"Oh! There they are," Tom stated as he had been scanning the room in search of his guests.

I was admittedly perplexed over the issue. Who are these people I will be meeting, Tom?

"You'll see!" Tom replied.

Tom disappeared for a few minutes around the corner of the lounge to apparently greet some guests. As I stood alone I watched my fellow students and their families engage in a celebration of love. I remember the proud smiles, the warm embraces and the chatter of congratulations. It was a happy time for everyone including the family and friends of those who endured previous suffering. It all felt so good. The energy was powerful even as I looked on as an outsider not interacting with anyone. I recalled the sacrifice I made in relationship to my family and I accepted it. And now I was ready to press forth with my life in a different direction if need be. I was finally ready. However, as confident as I felt there was one situation that could stand to test my readiness. And little did I know that Tom was about to bring forth the ultimate challenge.

"I believe you have all met before! Tom shouted as he returned from his muse around the lounge.

In his return he was standing beside a beautiful young woman and a little girl both dressed in summery attire. I was in a state of disbelief. You could even call it shock. Not a word came out of my mouth, as I stood before them speechless.

Dumfounded and surprised at the same time I was mostly scared. Despite the upstart of emotions that had come over me I didn't have the slightest inclination of what I would say if I could talk. Before me, in my flabbergasted quandary Tom had somehow reunited me with the wife I so dearly loved and the daughter that I tragically longed to hold. The two most important beings that I walked out on in my life were the same two that instantly walked into mine.

I had a tough time trying to find something to say. Oh my god you both look absolutely stunning!

"You look like you are doing pretty well yourself, Michael. I understand that you have had quite a journey the last little while!" Lisa said.

My lord I don't know what to say. I am speechless!

"You don't need to say anything, Michael!"

I don't?

"No, just give me a hug!" Lisa replied.

I guess if the hugs are going around I had better give you one too sweetie! I said as I both kissed and hugged my daughter.

While I was holding my daughter I was in a state that is beyond what any words could possibly describe. I had a smile as big as the moon as I turned to Tom and gave him a big wet kiss on the cheek. In doing so my daughter spoke. It was something I had yet to bear witness too since my departure from their lives. She managed to utter the words "I missed you daddy!"

They were few but powerful words that exploded in the confines of my heart. The tears streamed down my face in joy. I was so surprised over the whole notion that perhaps my wife and daughter could still be a part of my life. However, one question remained unanswered. How did Tom coordinate the reunion with Lisa and Eva?

I turned to Tom in search of some form of answer as to how it all came together. Unfortunately, he looked at me with a huge smile and laughed as he shrugged his shoulders in amazement at his act of kindness.

I was gleaming with happiness. I believed that I could honestly admit that I had finally found happiness! How did you pull it off behind my back?

"In all honesty I didn't," Tom replied.

What do you mean by that?

Tom motioned to Lisa. "May I steal Michael for a couple of minutes, please."

In making his request Tom took me several steps away from my wife and daughter. "Michael! You may have believed you walked out on your wife and daughter several months ago but you should be able to see it differently now."

I can see that physically I walked out on the two people that meant the most in my life but I would have to say that we never lost the connection between our hearts.

"That's because you didn't!" Tom replied.

I am beginning to witness firsthand the power of the universe, Tom.

"Now you know that we are all a part of the same energy that is perfectly connected through a means other than just the physical sense."

It all came together with the efforts of the universe?

"It all happened because it was suppose to happen, Michael. You never lost the connection in all your time apart in the spiritual sense. Your wife and daughter have been with you the entire time. They never let you go!"

Oh my god! I admitted in amazement.

"See the bigger picture, Michael?"

I see everything you have been talking about, I said excited for the first time in what felt like years.

It has been an educating experience for me, Tom.

"Education is a process of self-discovery, a defining of life values, a time of exploring and an unfolding of personal possibilities."

I tend to agree with you!

"The probability of science in your case, Michael, would tell us that you should have failed in your life journey thus far. However, your commitment to a higher vision has rallied you to restore what is essentially the real you."

I can see that finally, I admitted to Tom.

"In contrast to the idea of you failing you have proven to be a beacon of possibility in building a balance for the future and your exciting new voyage."

I look forward to it, Tom.

"If you ask me what has initiated such a dynamic, to identify the presence behind your energy, I would only suggest that it is not about how to do something, but the deep appreciation for the why of doing."

I see!

"Michael, it is not about achieving the so-called ideals of success, but rather the congruency of your actions with the principles you have learned. What is the purpose? To understand the nature of your tremendous inner power! To recognize and appreciate integrating consistency in the words and actions that reflect your true values and philosophy."

My true self!

"Exactly, Michael! You've got the 'bigger picture' down to a science."

I am so happy right know! I said to Tom.

"Isn't that what you told me you have wanted all along, Michael? To finally find happiness within yourself and in your life?"

Absolutely! I can't even remember what happiness was until today, I admitted to Tom.

"Michael, for what its worth I want you to hear my definition of happiness." Sure!

"Happiness is when you have something meaningful to look forward too."

I totally understand your view of happiness especially now that I can see the bigger picture.

"I know Michael! That's why I haven't told you until now. I wanted you to feel it so you could ultimately see it and be it. And you have done just that."

Lisa and my daughter looked remarkably different to me at that moment. It was as if I was seeing the vibration of the energy inside them. I saw a pulsating, bright red light inside of them both. My daughter had been growing so fast. She appeared shy as she remained very close to Lisa's side. She was as beautiful as I could have remembered. Her auburn colored hair, her big brown eyes. She was the spitting image of Lisa.

In all that had happened in those few short minutes I overwhelmingly felt that my heart was resurrected with the energy that it had lost over the years. And a part of my soul sank as I looked into the eyes of my wife and uttered an apology. Lisa stopped me in the process of apologizing by saying that she understood what was going on in my life. Lisa indicated that Dr. Marshall and Tom had informed her of the events of my destructive past. From the outset Lisa had spoken regularly with all of the parties concerned with my recovery.

There wasn't a detail that Lisa required an answer for. In fact, she knew the last several months of my life better than I. It was Tom's efforts that enabled us to reunite once again. It was clear what Tom had meant when he said to me that the players are in place. Of course it was also the most nerve-racking detail remaining. The task of confronting my wife and daughter in the near future despite the new person I had become. Tom obviously knew it was the greatest test for my personal development and wouldn't let me do it alone. For that I couldn't even begin to thank him. The other half of my heart was back at least for the time being.

Lisa looked at my weeping eyes. "I know everything thanks to Tom, Michael."

Everything Lisa?

"Everything!" She replied.

It has been quite an ordeal the last little while I have to admit.

"You are lucky to be standing here."

I wouldn't have known that until coming to the center, Lisa.

"You still have a long journey ahead of you I imagine, Michael."

I am very much aware of what lies ahead for me!

Lisa's voice took a soft yet serious tone.

"It's a journey that I don't want to see you travel alone!"

What? I said in disbelief.

"We haven't been apart from you, Michael. You have always been right here in our hearts."

And you in mine Lisa.

The tears began rolling down Lisa's face. "Please, if you will let us we would like to stay there for the rest of your life, Michael!"

I was motionless despite all of the excitement. Frozen in time.

"We came here today because I understood that the world was telling me it was the right time to reconnect with you, Michael."

I know we had always maintained a spiritual bond despite the direction I chose.

"I now know that you have found what you have spent years of your life searching for, Michael."

You do?

"Your journey is my journey and your daughters too. We all share in it together!" She replied. "Today symbolizes 'a new beginning' for our entire family, Michael!"

You mean together?

Lisa wrapped her arms around me. "Together, Michael!"

I must be dreaming or something.

"You, me and your daughter are going to walk out of the center together! Today! And we are never going to look back when we do!" Lisa stated with conviction."

We are going home together? I asked again in disbelief.

"Yes, together, Michael!" She stated firmly.

Are you sure you have thought all of it through?

"I have never been more sure of anything in my entire life. I wasn't sure I could understand the road you have traveled the last little while, Michael, but I know what it was you were in search of."

You do?

"Yes, Tom filled us in on most of the questions I had regarding your life and I believe that you needed that time to see life differently. More importantly I never left you during that journey, Michael. I have always sensed that I have been with you along the way. Together again we will start a new chapter in our lives if you will allow it."

My heart is a place that I have feared because it speaks of who I truly am as a spiritual entity. Today is a new beginning for us and of course I would love to have the two of you in my life again.

I was overcome by some emotions that I had never experienced before. Mostly because I believed they were the same ones that I had covered up in fear for most of my life. Finally, I had revealed my true self to the world. I felt vulnerable of the new experience yet amazed by its power. I was ecstatic that my wife and daughter still loved me despite my unnecessary actions of the past. It was all the perfect setting for a new beginning. And Tom wasn't kidding about how it would feel. I was so undeniably happy!

During the flood of emotions I suddenly noticed that Tom had ventured away from our celebration. He was nowhere to be seen physically although his spiritual energy was still existent. I was deeply indebted to him and all that he had done for me over the 'Eight Days in May' that we had spent together. I was just hoping for one last opportunity to thank him in person.

The experiences of triumphing over the perceived tragedies of my life were exhilarating. However, the most of uplifting feeling of all came from the time I spent traveling within. Coming to reacquaint myself with the power within. My inner being with the ability to connect to the depths of my heart! I realized that I had to acknowledge the messages of my heart in order to let my innate self shine through. It wasn't until I surrendered to the realization that the answers I had been searching for already resided inside my heart. And just as Tom had reminded me they truly were all I would ever need.

I was no doubt excited about the new beginning that had been bestowed upon me. The reconnection with my wife and daughter both spiritually and physically was incredibly powerful. The new beginning I was about to embark on had more meaning now that all the key players were in place. For the first time ever the 'Last Day In May' signified the first day of my new life. A life that I began to fully express from the heart! It was a new page in my life. A new chapter in my everlasting journey! A new beginning that had taken place in transforming my life and my world hand-in-hand. In opening my eyes and my heart I came to see life from a completely different vantage point. It had also become my reality in the manner in which it was designed. That of one world, one life, one message and one purpose! It finally made sense to me because I felt it inside. Because I was a part of it all along but just never knew it. And it can be yours too. If you just take the time to look deep inside!

Final Reflection

"Wise is the one who sees with his own eyes and listens with his own heart."
-Albert Einstein-

When I went to leave the center with my wife and daughter we passed the front desk area. The staff wished me one last goodbye and requested the return of my identification badge. Pulling the badge from my pant pocket I would never forget the way I felt the day Tom took that picture. I vividly remembered him mentioning that I would never recognize the person in the photo when I left the center. So before I returned the card I took one last moment to examine the former image.

I approached a full sized mirror in the lobby area. As I did I looked at myself and then the picture on the identification card. Astonished by what I saw Tom's words were true. I could barely decipher the difference between the two images. The picture looked nothing like the image in the mirror. Simply put there was no comparison. The image I saw in the mirror was far and away something I had never truly seen before. My true self.

You see I came to accept that the card revealed a lost soul trapped in a lifeless body. The newest image I saw in the mirror presented a deeper look. It was my inner power from the inside-out that I was finally able to see. The first glimpse of my body and my soul. Admittedly, I was taken aback but realized it would take some getting use to. Nonetheless, I was excited about the place I was living from in that moment. As I motioned toward the front desk I told Louisa that she could have the photo back. I mentioned to her that I couldn't quite make out who the person in it was anyway. Louisa quickly refuted that the picture was my initial photo taken the day I started in the program. No, I told her! I knew in that moment that the picture was of someone I once thought I knew.

I had committed to leading and living my life from a much better place through my workings with Tom. An undertaking that I fully intended to see through. After reminding myself of the intentions I had regarding the awakening I had experienced I asked Louisa to do me one last favor. I requested that she not destroy the card. And I reached for a sticky note and a pen that was on her desk. And I began writing a message. The message read:

Tom,
You were right! When I looked at this picture for the last time I finally understood what you meant when you said you saw something trapped on the inside. My power from the inside can now be seen and used on the outside. Thank you! I will be forever greatful for the "Eight Days In May."

I stuck the note on the picture card and handed it to Louisa. She promised me she would give it to Tom the minute she saw him. As I bid the staff one last good-bye I took a quick scan of the center for Tom and motioned for the front entrance. As we walked outside I could feel the gusts of the warm summer breeze. In that instant an innate sense spoke to me. I knew exactly where that crazy coach of mine was. He would be gracing the shores of his office looking for the next best wave. In fact, I could even hear him shouting and laughing as he rode the wave before plunging into the ocean in anticipation of the next "big one."

The "Eight Days In May" allowed me to plunge so to speak into understanding what, who and where "I" really had been in the experience called life. And for anyone who decides to take the inward journey the powerful lessons from the "Eight Days In May" can help you to discover all of the answers you will ever need to lead you to the extra-ordinary life you've been searching for. You see life itself has been confused with being a "success story." When truly life as it was meant to be lived is really just a "love story" from the heart..

Printed in the United States
76244LV00003B/13-144